Don't Look Back

Lily's Story, Book 2

Books by Christine Kersey

Lily's Story Trilogy

He Loves Me Not (Lily's Story, Book 1)
Don't Look Back (Lily's Story, Book 2)
Love At Last (Lily's Story, Book 3)

Parallel Trilogy

Gone (Parallel Trilogy, Book 1)
Imprisoned (Parallel Trilogy, Book 2)
Hunted (Parallel Trilogy, Book 3)
Morgan and Billy, a Parallel Trilogy story — coming May, 2014
The Other Morgan, a Parallel Trilogy story — coming August, 2014

Over You — 2 book series

Over You
Sequel to *Over You — coming March, 2014*

Standalone Books

Suspicions
No Way Out

Don't Look Back (Lily's Story, Book 2)

Visit Christine's blog: christinekersey.blogspot.com

Don't Look Back

Lily's Story, Book 2

Christine Kersey

Wind Chimes Publishing

Chapter One

I stood on the gravel driveway gazing at the house I wanted to live in, the *For Rent* sign in the front window seeming to call to me. Blue shutters framed the windows and colorful pansies lined the walkway leading to the wide front porch. It matched the house I had pictured whenever I had imagined the perfect place to live. The only thing missing was the picket fence.

Excitement pulsed through me as I pictured myself living there with my baby. But the excitement was replaced by worry that the rent would be too high. Though I had eighty-five thousand dollars to draw on, I had no immediate prospects for a job and needed the money to last as long as possible.

But I needed to find a place to settle. I had to try.

Hurrying back to my car, I pulled my new cell phone out of my purse and called the number listed on the For Rent sign. Disappointed to get voice mail, I left a message and put the phone in my pocket.

I walked toward the rear of the house, through a gate, and found a back porch. A door appeared to lead to the kitchen, and a window in the top half of the door made it easy to peek inside. The small kitchen held a breakfast nook and looked like it had plenty of cupboards. I walked around the outside of the house but the rest of the windows had curtains and I couldn't see inside.

Going back to the front porch, I looked through the living room window and saw a small room with hardwood floors and a fireplace. As I walked back toward my car my cell phone rang, startling me. Afraid the caller might somehow be my husband, Trevor, I pulled the phone out of my pocket and looked at the caller ID. It was a local area code.

Hopeful it would be the owner of the house, I pressed the button to connect. "Hello?"

"Is this the person who called about the house?" The woman's voice sounded friendly.

"Yes. Is it still available?"

"Oh yes."

"That's great! I'm at the house now. Would it be possible for me to take a look inside?"

The woman spoke to someone in the background, then to me. "I'll be there in a few minutes."

Promising to wait, I closed my phone, then realized I'd forgotten to ask about the rent. Frowning, I sat on the porch.

Fifteen minutes later I was getting worried that the woman wasn't going to come. The warmth of the spring day was beginning to get to me and I wondered how much longer I should wait.

I glanced at the clock on my cell phone, then heard a car approaching. Looking toward the road, I was relieved when I saw a car turning into the gravel drive, then pull to a stop. I watched as an older woman climbed out of the car and made her way toward me.

Standing as the woman approached, I smiled.

"I'm so sorry I'm late," the woman said, then glanced around. "Is it just you, dear?"

I smiled. "Yep, just me."

"Oh, I see."

"I'd really like to see the inside of the house, if that's okay." Her reaction to me being on my own made me worry that she wouldn't be willing to rent the house to me.

The woman suddenly smiled and held out her hand. "I'm Mary."

I shook Mary's hand, my fears easing.

"Kate. Kate Jamison." It felt strange to introduce myself with that name, but I knew I would need to get used to it since I had decided to use that name instead of my real name, Lily, to make it harder for Trevor to find me.

She pointed to my car. "I see you're from Nevada. I lived there for a while myself."

"Oh. How long have you lived in California?"

"About thirty years, I guess." Mary paused. "How old are you, dear?"

"I'll be twenty-one next month."

"And your parents don't mind you moving all the way here by yourself?"

I bit my lip, startled by the question. "I don't know how they would feel. They're both . . . dead." I swallowed hard to keep the tears from starting.

Mary placed her hand on my arm. "I'm so sorry to hear that. How sad for you."

Nodding, I tried to smile.

"Well, let's take a look inside, shall we?" Mary pulled a key from her pocket and unlocked the door, then stepped back to allow me to enter first.

The interior was stuffy from being closed up on a warm day, but I still liked the feel of the place. It was a small house—more like a two-story cottage—but it was clean. I walked around the empty living room and noticed it could use a coat of paint, but it was big enough for me. Mary must have thought it need to be painted as well, because she said I could paint it if I'd like.

There was a combination half-bath/laundry room off of the hall that led to the kitchen. Having my own laundry room would be quite a luxury.

"The washer and dryer are older, but they work," Mary said.

We moved into the U-shaped kitchen. It was medium-sized and looked like it had plenty of storage and counter space. Even better, the appliances were all there. Adjacent to the kitchen was a small dining room.

"This house has been here for a long time," Mary said as I followed her from room to room. "My husband and I bought it and lived here when we first moved to California. We quickly outgrew it of course. But we decided to hang on to it."

"How many bedrooms are there?" I asked as we ascended the narrow staircase.

"Just the two."

At the top of the stairs I turned right, which was the only way to go. I walked down the hallway and turned left, into the larger of the two bedrooms. Like the rest of the house, it had hardwood floors. There were two windows—one each on two separate walls.

"Lots of natural light," Mary pointed out.

I nodded as I walked out of the bedroom and peeked into the small bathroom situated next to the master bedroom. Then I stepped across the hall into the second bedroom and could immediately picture a crib along one wall and a dresser and changing table against the other.

"This would be perfect for the baby," I murmured.

"Baby? What baby?" Mary asked.

Alarmed that I had spoken out loud, I wasn't sure what to say.

"Are you pregnant, dear?" Mary asked, glancing at my left ring finger.

Grateful I had decided to leave my wedding ring on, I nodded.

"Will the baby's father be living here too?"

Panicked that if I gave out too much information Trevor would somehow find me, I hesitated. "No. He's no longer . . . around."

"What do you mean? Is he . . . dead?"

Somehow, at that moment, it seemed easier to let the woman believe I was a widow. I nodded.

"You poor thing. You've certainly had your share of tragedy, now haven't you?"

Thinking about the last year and the loss of my father, and my bad marriage to Trevor and how he had treated me, lied to me and about me, I couldn't hold back the tears. It was like a damn bursting and I pressed my hands to my eyes to try to stop the flow.

Suddenly I felt Mary, the woman I had barely met, wrap her arms around me. The empathy I felt from her made me sob even harder. After a few minutes I was able to get myself under control. Wiping the tears from my face, I straightened and faced Mary. "I'm sorry. I didn't mean to lose control like that."

"That's okay, dear. Sometimes we need to have a good cry."

I nodded as she ushered me back down the stairs and onto the front porch.

"Thank you for showing me the house," I said, feeling calmer.

"Well, do you like it?"

"Very much, but I'm afraid I probably can't afford it."

"How do you know that when I haven't even told you how much the rent is?"

"Well, I can only imagine how much it would be. And I just don't think it would fit my budget." I smiled again, trying to hide my disappointment. "But thank you for coming all the way out here and showing it to me."

"Young lady, I do believe we can work something out." Mary smiled with kindness. "I'd like to see you live here. I think you would take good care of this old place." She paused. "Tell me how much you have budgeted for rent."

I told her the most I felt comfortable paying.

"Well that seems fair to me. And the peace of mind I would have in knowing my property is in good hands has value too."

"Really? Are you sure?" I could hardly believe my good fortune.

"Look. This place is paid for. And the last few tenants didn't love the place like I know you will."

"Thank you so much. You have no idea how much this means to me." I gently stroked my flat stomach. "To both of us."

Mary arranged to meet me back at the house the next morning so I could sign the rental agreement and pay the first month's rent along with a security deposit.

As I drove back to the motel, I paid careful attention to where I was so I could find my way back the next day.

CHAPTER TWO

As I lay in bed that night, I wondered what Trevor was doing at that very moment. Was he thinking about me? Was he plotting how to find me? Was he still in jail or had his friend Bronson bailed him out? How had he reacted when he'd discovered I'd taken back the money he'd stolen from me? What was he telling his parents about his new wife and why I had left? Was he still trying to convince them it was me who had a drinking problem and not him? Perhaps he had told them I had gone on a binge and left in a drunken stupor and he didn't know where I was or when I'd be back.

As I thought about the lies he had told about me, I seethed with anger. He had tricked me, plain and simple. It was true that from the start he had never portrayed himself as the perfect man, but he certainly hadn't told me that he was a thief and a liar either.

He also didn't tell me he had such a temper. Or was it my fault he behaved that way? Did I set him off each time? Could I have done something different to prevent his outbursts and jealousy?

I closed my eyes and shook my head. *It's not my fault. I'm the same person I've always been and no one has ever hurt me like that. That is, until Trevor.*

I wondered if I would always have bad judgment when it came to men.

It doesn't matter anyway, I thought. I have no desire to get involved with anyone ever again. Besides, technically I'm still married. And the only thing I want to focus on is myself and my baby. That's all that matters now.

I finally drifted off to sleep, but near morning I woke abruptly from a nightmare. Trevor had found me and locked me up again. But this time there was an added terror—he had taken my baby.

Not able to fall back asleep, I got up and showered, packed my belongings, and checked out of the motel. I tried to shake off the lingering fear the nightmare had generated and instead focused on the possibilities that my future held.

Driving around the small town in the early morning dawn, I thought I was going to like living here. The downtown was hardly more than two rows of stores lining the street. Although there weren't a lot of shops, the area was quite pretty. Trees seemed to march up and down the street, and bricks formed crosswalks at each corner.

No one was around this early in the morning, but I had time to kill so I pulled my car into a parking space and climbed out. As I walked the short distance from one end of the street to the other, I looked in the store windows. When I came to a bakery I stopped, seeing a Help Wanted sign prominently displayed in the window. I wondered if I had any chance of getting a job there. I could see people working inside. I decided to apply once I had moved my few belongings into my new house.

Checking the time, I saw it was close enough to the time I had agreed to meet Mary at the house and decided to head over there. Five minutes later I pulled up to the little cottage and felt a thrill at the prospect of living there. Although I didn't have any furniture, I was sure I could find some things at garage sales. In the meantime I would make do.

I didn't have long to wait until Mary came. This time she brought her husband, Edward. He was just as friendly as Mary.

"It sure is nice of you to give me a break on the rent," I said.

Edward smiled. "Mary told me about your situation and we're happy to help you out."

I felt a bit guilty that they believed I was a widow and I hoped that hadn't played too large a part in their decision to cut the rent. Though I felt sorry for the lie, I knew I hadn't done it to purposely fool anyone so much as to protect myself and my unborn child.

When they presented the rental agreement, I hesitated. Should I sign my name as Lily or Kate? They hadn't asked to see an ID, so I went ahead and signed as Kate Jamison, making my deception complete. I handed the paper back to them and they didn't question it. I gave them the first month's rent and the security deposit in cash, and they gave me the key.

"The utilities were never turned off. You'll just need to put them in your name," Edward said. "By the way, when is the moving truck arriving?"

I felt my face color. "Actually, this is it." I pointed to my car.

"What about your furniture?" Mary asked, concern clear on her face.

"Oh, I'm sure I'll be able to find what I need."

"You mean you're buying all new things?" Mary asked, obviously shocked by the idea of such an extravagance.

"Oh no," I said. "I'll hit the garage sales. And isn't there a Goodwill around here somewhere?"

"Yes, there's one in the next town."

"Great. I'll check it out." I smiled. "And thank you again for your kindness."

They left after that and I was able to begin moving my things into the house. As I hung my belongings on the few hangers that had been left in the closet, I wondered what would be comfortable to sleep on that night.

I could buy an air mattress and sleeping bag, I thought. It would be like the campouts Dad used to take me on.

I smiled in sweet remembrance of the good times I had shared with my father, then felt a pang of guilt for depriving my own child the company of his or her father. But as I thought of the harm Trevor could do by treating me so poorly in front of our child, I felt my remorse vanish. I knew I was doing the right thing. I knew it more clearly than I had ever known anything in my life. Nodding in grim satisfaction that I was making the right choice, I headed back out to my car and brought in the rest of my things.

As I placed the few pieces of my mother's china that I had been able to salvage from Trevor's fit of rage in the cupboard, I felt peace to have a small bit of my childhood home in my new home. Once the last plate was placed on the shelf, I stood back and surveyed my kitchen.

Though there was plenty of cabinet and counter space, I didn't have anything with which to fill the drawers and cupboards. The china had only taken up half of one cupboard. Worry washed over me as I considered the expense it would take to get the minimal necessities.

Pressing my hands to my face, I felt despair threatening my earlier feeling of peace.

What does it matter what I have, I thought, lifting my face and gazing at my new backyard. As long as I'm safe and have my freedom, it doesn't matter what *things* I have.

As my innate optimism cleansed away my despair, I heard a knock at the door and froze, suddenly terrified that Trevor had tracked me down. Frantically glancing around for some place to hide, I realized that I was vulnerable in this house, away from so many other people.

"Kate?" someone was shouting. "Are you okay?"

Relief surged through me as I recognized Mary's voice. Hurrying to the door, I was shocked to see what she had brought.

CHAPTER THREE

There were two pickup trucks parked in the driveway, both full of furniture. My eyes met Mary's. "What is this?"

Mary grinned. "When Edward and I saw you didn't have a stick of furniture, we knew just what to do. You see, our church has been collecting furniture and household goods to donate to charity. But we all agree that you could use it the most." She paused. "I hope you don't mind, dear."

Trying to control the tears that were pushing their way into my eyes, I shook my head. "I don't mind at all."

"Good. Then let these nice men get to work and move you in."

I stepped onto the porch with Mary by my side as the men began carrying in all the furniture, towels, sheets, and dishes I could have wished for. It didn't take long for them to finish, and I could only smile in gratitude. I knew if I opened my mouth to thank them I would burst into tears.

When the men had left and only Mary remained, I hugged the old woman. "You must be the kindest person I've ever met."

"Thank you, dear," Mary said, as I released her. "It was worth it just to see the expression on your face." She chuckled. "To say you were surprised would be an understatement."

I laughed. "At first when I heard the knock on the door I thought it was . . ." I stopped abruptly, realizing I had almost given away my secret.

"Thought it was what, dear?"

"I thought it was a sales person."

"Oh, I wouldn't worry too much about that. Most sales people don't want to bother coming out here."

"That's one benefit of living in the country, I guess."

"One of many. You'll find it's very quiet at night. Only the sound of the crickets to keep you company. I hope you don't mind the solitude."

"Not at all. I actually grew up in a small town, so this isn't all that different."

"Good. Well you have a nice day, Kate. And give me a call if you need anything."

After assuring her that I would, I waved good bye, then went back into my house to see what the men had brought.

There was a couch, end table, and coffee table in the living room, a small table with chairs in the dining room, and a bed and dresser in my bedroom. Fresh sheets and towels were stacked on the dresser and a blanket was folded neatly on the bed.

Overwhelmed with gratitude, I had never felt so loved before. Any lingering doubt about my choice to leave Trevor had been completely erased.

Inspecting my kitchen, I found several boxes that held dishes and other kitchen items. However, there were still a few things I would need to buy to make my kitchen functional. I also needed to make a big trip to the grocery store to stock up on staples, like flour, sugar, and the like. But first I would open an account at the bank and deposit the money I'd brought with me.

The eighty-five thousand dollars was all I had left from my father's life insurance policy and it was vital to my survival. I didn't feel comfortable having that kind of cash lying around the house, unprotected. That money would pay for my education and I would need every penny to see me through the next few years it would take to complete my degree.

I also realized I would most likely have to sell Dad's house sooner than I had planned. But before making that decision, I would rely on the cash on hand.

Though I planned on getting a job, I was realistic enough to know that once the baby was born, working and going to school would be extremely difficult. I had to conserve my funds now in order to ensure I could survive once the baby came.

As I thought about the most recent semester and how close I had come to finishing it, my anger at Trevor rekindled. When I'd become pregnant and had tried to leave, he had found me and brought me home, then locked me in our apartment and not allowed me to finish the semester. There had only been two weeks left, but his fear that I would run had given him the excuse he needed to prevent me from going anywhere or seeing anyone.

When I had convinced him I was happy with him and would never leave, he had left me on my own and I had called the police with a tip that he was involved in the recent car thefts that had been occurring in the area. The next thing I knew, he had been arrested and I had taken advantage of the opportunity and run.

Now I was here in this small town in the Central Valley of California, relishing my freedom, yet wary of anyone knowing the truth about my past.

Besides the fear of Trevor finding me, I felt ashamed—ashamed that I had been so easily fooled. Trevor must have seen me as an easy mark. Maybe he did love me, but he had also stolen the money my father had left me. I felt stupid for trusting him, for falling for him, for believing he loved me.

Pushing aside the mistakes from the past, I picked up my purse and went out to my car. After stopping by the bank and opening an account, I drove to the bakery. The Help Wanted sign was still there and since things were going so well today, I had high hopes I would be able to get this job. My hopes were quickly dashed, however, when the owner of the bakery told me she wanted someone with more experience.

"But I learn quickly and I'm a hard worker," I said.

"I'm sorry, but I just don't think you're right for the job."

Embarrassed to have the few customers in the store watch my rejection, I left the bakery and walked back toward my car.

Chapter Four

Though feeling dejected, I decided to go to the grocery store. I ended up driving to the next town over, since my town was too small to have anything more than mom and pop stores and I wanted the selection and pricing of the large stores.

As I walked up and down the aisles, I thought about Mary and how she and her husband believed I had been widowed. While I felt bad about misleading them, I knew it was best for people to know as little as possible about my situation. The less they knew, the less likely someone would say something that would lead Trevor to me. The thought of Trevor tracking me down terrified me. I knew he would feel I had betrayed him when I didn't come to the jail and bail him out. He had trusted me to bring the gym bag full of *my* money to the jail. He'd had no one else to turn to and I had let him down. At least I was sure that would be how he would see it.

Then I remembered what he'd said the last time he had threatened me about running away. I pictured the cold look in his eyes as he'd warned me, *If I have to track you down again there are going to be some serious consequences.* I didn't know what those 'consequences' would be, but if they were more serious than keeping me prisoner in my own home, I didn't want to know what he had in mind.

As different scenarios flashed through my mind, all feelings of security fled and I felt a strong urge to run. My gaze darted wildly from one shopper to the next, but they were oblivious to me, busy choosing items from the shelves and placing them in their carts. No one paid attention to me and I took several deep breaths, trying to calm myself.

He has no idea where you are, I thought, as I reached for a can of soup, my hand shaking. For all you know, he's in jail and will be there for a long time. He'll eventually lose interest in you and you'll be home free.

I tried to believe those ideas, but deep down I knew he would never stop looking for me. Hopelessness cascaded over me and it felt like someone had placed a heavy jacket around my shoulders. A jacket that weighed me down and made it difficult to move forward.

I had always had an optimistic attitude, but the thoughts I was having were difficult to overcome. By strength of will, I kept walking down the aisle, studiously following my list and filling my cart with what I needed. I was grateful I had the list—I was having trouble thinking clearly and felt certain I wouldn't have a clue what to buy if it wasn't written down.

Finally finished checking off all the items on my list, I trudged to the checkout line and purchased my groceries. After loading the bags into my car, I pulled out of my parking space and drove toward the exit.

Activity on a grassy area near the exit caught my eye. A group of people were surrounding something. I watched as a man bent down, then stood back up, a puppy in his hands. I drove my car toward the group, parking in a space nearby. I watched the activity for a few minutes, seeing the happy faces of the people playing with the puppies. A gap in the group opened up and I counted three puppies. They looked like German Shepherd puppies.

I'd always heard that German Shepherds made excellent watch dogs. I imagined Trevor knocking down my front door and my dog protecting me. I opened my car door and was walking toward the puppies before I had completed visualizing the possible incident with Trevor.

I watched the other people as they played with the puppies. "How are they with children?" I asked the owner.

He looked at me and smiled, a puppy in his arms. "How old is the kid?"

"A baby," I said, not wanting to elaborate.

"Well, it's always a good idea to not leave babies alone with any dog, but German Shepherds are good with kids."

He held out the puppy for me to take. I took the puppy and asked how old it was.

"She's eight weeks."

She felt substantial in my arms and I felt more secure just having her against me. "How much?"

"Two hundred."

I tried not to flinch at the price. I knew that even though you could get some puppies for free, others could be pricey. I held her away from me and gazed at her sweet face. When her gaze met mine, she seemed to be telling me that she would protect me. Even though I hadn't owned a pet before, I was certain I could learn whatever I needed to know. She would be my family now.

"I'd like to buy this one," I said, setting the puppy back in the enclosure.

As I pulled out my checkbook, the man said, "Sorry, but I only take cash."

"Oh sure. Okay." I tucked my checkbook away. "Can you hold on to her for me while I run to the bank?"

"No problem. What's your name?"

"Li . . . uh, Kate." I felt my face begin to redden as I caught myself almost using my real name.

"I can hold her for an hour."

I smiled, covering my near mistake. "Great. I'll be back in a few minutes."

Walking quickly to my car, I drove to the bank and withdrew the needed money, then drove back and bought my new puppy.

"What are you going to call her?" the man asked.

"Hmm. I'm not sure." I looked at the puppy's face again. "Well, since you're a *German* Shepherd, how about Greta?" I waited a moment, hoping the dog would bark or give some other indication that I had chosen the right name, but she just looked at me. But it almost seemed like she was smiling. "Yes, I'll call you Greta."

"Well, you enjoy her. I know you'll be happy with her."

I held Greta against me and smiled at the man. "Thanks."

As I walked back to my car I held Greta close. "We'll need to get you some supplies." I had noticed a pet supply store as I was driving to the grocery store and decided to go there. I carefully climbed into the car, Greta in my arms, and shut the door. "Now, how are we going to do this?" I set her on the passenger seat, but wasn't sure how I could keep her from falling to the floor if I had to stop suddenly. Then I lifted her from the seat and placed her on the floor instead. I gently pressed her into a laying position and she stayed that way.

Snapping my seatbelt on, I started the car and carefully drove out of the parking lot. In only a few minutes I had pulled into a parking space at the pet supply store. By this time Greta was standing. After I turned off the car I leaned toward her and lifted her into my arms. Carrying her into the store, I found a store employee and explained that I had just bought the puppy and didn't have any supplies. He grabbed a shopping cart and helped me pick out everything I would need. Then he pushed the cart to the register and I paid for my purchases. I set Greta in the cart, on top of a pet bed, and pushed it out to my car.

My trunk was already pretty full of groceries, but I fit what I could into the trunk. Then I put the pet bed on the floor in front of the passenger seat and placed Greta on top, then loaded the rest of the items onto the backseat.

"Whew!" I said, looking at Greta. "That's a lot of stuff."

This time she barked in response to my voice and I felt like we were becoming friends.

I drove back to my new home and brought Greta inside, then took several trips to unload everything else. After setting the last bag of groceries on the kitchen counter, I noticed a small puddle on the kitchen floor.

"Oh no." I dug through the grocery bags and found the paper towels, then quickly cleaned up the mess. When that was done, I pulled out the book on German Shepherds that I'd bought at the pet supply store. Then, opening the door to the backyard, I called to Greta to come with me. She scampered after me and onto the grass. I watched her explore the large backyard as I sat on the steps of the back porch, flipping through the book. After a moment I found the section on house training.

Over the next several hours I worked with Greta on teaching her to go to the bathroom outside. I hadn't realized how exhausting this was going to be, but I knew the hard work would pay off eventually.

That afternoon as I walked her outside, it occurred to me that Mary and Edward might not approve of me having a dog in their house. I decided to call them and hope for the best. I pulled out my cell phone and called Mary. I hung up a short time later, relieved that Mary had not only approved of the dog, but thought it was a good idea since I was living here by myself.

I smiled at Greta as she jumped up on me, begging for attention. "I think we need to send you to obedience school." I reached down and scratched her head, which made her tail wag in apparent happiness. I picked up the ball I had bought and tossed it across the yard. Greta shot out after it and then trotted back, the ball in her mouth. We did this for about fifteen minutes until I had to stop and take a break.

Sitting down on the porch steps again, I watched Greta drink out of her water bowl, then smiled as she flopped down in the shade. It felt good to have a companion and it felt even better to be able to forget about my problems for a while. But even as the thought entered my head, I couldn't help but catalogue my problems: Trevor becoming abusive, Trevor being arrested for stealing cars, Trevor locking me up, Trevor stealing from me and then me having to run and hide from Trevor.

Wow, I thought. Each and every problem involves Trevor. Less than a year ago I didn't know he existed, and now he was the root of all my problems. What was I going to do? I knew I couldn't hide from him forever.

I thought about my mild panic attack at the grocery store and knew I had to do all within my power to make sure I could protect myself. I looked over at Greta and smiled, knowing she was a good first defense. I knew I needed to get her trained as soon as she was ready. Otherwise she wouldn't be able to do much to protect me.

What if she can't protect me? Then what would I do? I pondered this for a few minutes, then I realized I could learn some self-defense. My pregnancy wasn't starting to show yet, so I was still in good physical shape to take a self-defense course.

I wanted to go online to look up information on dog training and self-defense, but I didn't have Internet access yet. First things first, I thought. I pulled out my cell phone and called information, asking them to connect me to the cable company for my area. A few minutes later I had made an appointment to have someone come out and hook up a cable connection for TV as well as a cable modem. Someone would be out the next day.

Chapter Five

That night, my first in my new house, I listened to every creak and groan the house made as I tried to go to sleep. I had made sure all the doors and windows were locked tight and Greta was curled up on her pet bed in a corner of my room, but still I couldn't help but feel a little nervous that somehow Trevor would find me. After a while, I finally fell asleep.

The next day as I was cleaning up from breakfast, someone knocked on the door. Even though I was expecting the cable company to come, I had to force myself to calm down before walking to the door and looking through the peephole. Relieved to see a stranger in a cable company uniform on the porch, I opened the door.

"Are you Kate Jamison?"

I nodded. "Yes. Please come in."

"This shouldn't take too long," he said as he followed me inside.

I watched him step into the living room and look around. I thought he wasn't much older than me, maybe in his late twenties.

"Where's your TV?" he asked as he turned toward me.

"I don't have one yet."

He laughed. "People usually have a TV before they have their cable set up."

Feeling foolish, I felt my face redden. "Well, I mostly want the Internet access, but your company had a deal going where I could get free cable for my TV."

"Oh. Well, that makes sense."

"Anyway, I'm planning on getting a TV soon. I just haven't gotten around to it yet."

"Your boyfriend will probably be glad when you get one."

"My boyfriend?" Slight panic tickled my neck.

He laughed again. "You do have a boyfriend, don't you?"

His question made me very uncomfortable. I didn't want him to know I lived here by myself. I held up my left ring finger and pointed to my wedding ring. "I don't have a boyfriend, but I do have a husband."

That made him back off.

"Well, just give me a little time to get this all hooked up and I'll be out of your way."

"Thanks."

I heard barking at the back door and let Greta in. She immediately ran up to the man and started sniffing him. I pulled her away. "Sorry. She gets a little excited sometimes."

"No problem," he said.

Half an hour later he said everything was hooked up and if I had any trouble, to give them a call.

"I usually like to test out the cable connection on the TV, but . . . "

I smiled. "That's okay. Thanks."

He left and I locked the door behind him, glad to be alone. His questions about my having a boyfriend had been unnerving. It made me wonder what I could do to make it less apparent that I lived alone.

I pulled out my laptop and plugged it into the modem. I was online in no time. The first thing I did was check my email. My heart pounded when I saw that my mailbox held several emails from Trevor. Hesitant to open them, I decided it would be a good idea to find out his mood. I knew just opening and reading the emails wouldn't help him find me.

The first few emails had a sweet and loving tone, asking me to come home and be a family with him. There was no mention of his arrest or that I had taken my money back. As I continued to read the emails, the persuasiveness turned to anger and threats. The final email had been sent just that morning. As I read it, I felt my mouth go dry.

Lily,

I know you think you're clever in running from me and taking my money, but be assured that I WILL find you. You're still my wife and you're carrying OUR child. I have every right to be a part of that child's life and I plan on seeing my child grow up. With or without you, I will be a father to my child.

You and I both know that you have NO ONE. You are on your own. NO ONE will help you. I hope you don't sleep at night for fear that I will be watching. I will know when you give birth to OUR baby. I WILL use my rights as the baby's father and I WILL take him and raise him. If you don't cooperate in allowing me to be a part of our baby's life, I will make sure that he will never know he had a mother.

Your LOVING husband,

Trevor

The fear that had pushed me to leave him came rushing back and I felt tears course down my cheeks as I knew he spoke the truth. I had no one. I was completely on my own.

But would he really be able to find me? Would he really take my baby from me? I wrapped my arms protectively around my abdomen. I was in no hurry to have this baby—as long as it was inside me, he couldn't take it from me.

He doesn't know where I am and he has no way to find me, I thought. I never got around to changing my last name to his. He doesn't know my social security number. He has no idea which way I headed when I left. For all he knows, I moved to New York.

Trying to think of any way he could possibly track me down, I felt reassured that I was safe. I just had to be careful. Feeling better, I saved all the emails Trevor had sent, but didn't reply. The rest of the emails were junk and I deleted them. I thought about my good friend Alyssa.

Right now, during the summer, she was probably with her parents and had no idea that I had left Trevor. Alyssa had tried to tell me that Trevor didn't seem like a good person, but I had stubbornly ignored her.

Pulling up a new email, I sent Alyssa a brief note telling her that I had left Trevor and I was doing fine. I explained that I couldn't tell her where I had gone, but I would keep in touch through email.

Next, I did a search for dog obedience schools in the area. I found one that would be starting the following week and signed up for it. Then I did a search for self-defense courses. The police department was offering a four-week course. I was worried that being pregnant would be a problem, but since I wasn't showing yet, I thought it would be okay. And the peace of mind I would have in knowing some self-defense moves would be worth it. I signed up for the course, excited to learn how to protect myself.

Finally, I found the website for the local junior college and pulled up the page to apply for fall admissions. I knew I could get one semester completed before the baby came and planned to make the most of the opportunity.

Once the admission process had been started, I felt excited at the thought of going to school.

That night, as I lay in bed, I replayed Trevor's email over and over. I knew he must be very angry with me. The thought of his anger directed at me was terrifying. Having seen his anger in action, I knew he was capable of hurting me. I glanced over at Greta, curled up in the corner, and hoped between her and the self-defense class, I'd be able to keep myself and my baby safe.

CHAPTER SIX

I found the park where the dog obedience lessons were going to take place and climbed out of the car. Greta tugged at her leash as we walked toward the group of dogs and owners. I smiled at the other owners as they tried to control their rambunctious puppies. Greta seemed calm in comparison and I smiled like a proud mother.

One woman with a black lab seemed to be having an especially hard time.

"No, Chloe," she said as the dog vigorously sniffed another owner.

I stifled a laugh, glad Greta wasn't quite that friendly.

"I'm so sorry," Chloe's owner said.

The other owner smiled, clearly uncomfortable.

"She's a beautiful dog," I said.

Chloe's owner turned to me. She looked like she was in her thirties and had a mass of curly brown hair held in place by two large barrettes. "Thanks. She's really sweet, just a little overly friendly sometimes."

"Well, that's why we're here, I guess."

"What's your dog's name?" the woman asked.

"Greta."

"She's a pretty dog too."

"Thanks."

"I'm Billi," the woman said.

"Nice to meet you. I'm Kate."

"Have you been to obedience school before?"

"No. In fact this is the first dog I've owned."

"Really?"

"What about you?" I asked, holding tightly to Greta's leash as she tried to get a a closer look at the other dogs.

"I've been through this once before. It really helped with my other dog."

"That's good to hear. I'm really hoping I can get Greta trained."

"Well, German Shepherds are really smart dogs, so I would imagine it shouldn't be too difficult."

We stopped talking as the instructor said he was ready to begin. An hour later I loaded Greta into my car, feeling pretty good about how well she had done. The next lesson would be the following week.

When we got home I played with her in the backyard for a while, then placed her in her crate before heading to the local paint store. Mary had given me permission to paint and I intended to put the stamp of my personality on my house.

I had a hard time deciding exactly which color to choose for the living room, but finally selected a blue-grey color. I also bought brushes and rollers and any other supplies I thought I would need. Fortunately I had painted before—when I lived with Dad we had painted several rooms in our house—so I knew what I was doing.

Excited to make the house my own, I hurried home, let Greta out of her crate, and set out my supplies. After dragging the couch into the middle of the small room, I laid out the drop cloth to protect the wood floor.

Greta immediately grabbed a corner and began dragging it, certain we were playing a game. I couldn't help but laugh. "No, Greta. This is for painting." I tugged on the drop cloth but that only made her pull harder. Suddenly the cloth ripped and Greta sat on her bottom with a thump. I laughed harder at the surprised look on her face.

She began shaking the fabric in her mouth like it was prey she was trying to kill.

26

"Okay. Enough of that." I gently removed it from her mouth. "Back in the crate with you." I put her back in her crate and repositioned the covering on the floor.

Greta barked, wanting to be with me, and I didn't know what to do. I hated for her to be unhappy, but I certainly couldn't paint if she was allowed to run loose. Her barks turned to whimpers. I went upstairs and got her pet bed and set it in the dining room where she'd be out of the way but still able to see me. Then I secured her leash to one of the legs on the dining room table and attached the other end to her collar. Setting a toy on her pet bed, I was able to get her to lay down.

I placed painting tape around the ceiling and baseboards, then I poured some paint into the tray, dipped the roller into the paint and started covering the wall. After covering a large area, I stepped back and admired my work. I loved the color—it relaxed me. Within an hour I had finished the first coat.

After cleaning up, I took Greta out back and watched her run around while I sat on the porch steps. I need to get a chair for back here, I thought, mentally adding it to my list of things to buy.

As I thought of the items I wanted to buy, I knew it would soon become critical that I have a job. I went inside and grabbed my laptop and brought it outside. The cable modem had a built-in router so I was able to access the Internet wirelessly.

I pulled up a job search website and looked for jobs in my area that I was qualified for. Most of the listings required a degree—not that I had the skills they wanted—but it soon became apparent that I would have to set my sights much lower. Pulling up the websites of local retailers, I filled out several online applications and submitted them, hoping for the best.

Next, I found the site for the Reno newspaper and searched for information on Trevor's arrest. There was a short article about two men being arrested for motor vehicle thefts, but it didn't list their names. I could only assume the article was about Trevor and Rob. Then I pulled up the website for the jail but couldn't find anything with Trevor's name. I saw several arrests, but the names were blocked for privacy reasons. I wondered if his was one of those.

In any case, he clearly was no longer in jail or he wouldn't have been able to email me. Every time I thought about him searching for me, panic engulfed me. What if he found me? Would he hurt me, or try to convince me to be with him? The unknown scared me more than anything.

Later that evening I painted the second coat on the living room walls. Pleased with the results, I decided to work on the nursery next. First thing the next morning I went back to the paint store and picked out a soft green paint. I figured that color would work for a boy or a girl.

Once home, I carried the supplies up to the baby's room. Since there was no furniture, this would be a perfect time to paint. I put Greta in her crate downstairs and she didn't bark this time. I assumed it was because I was upstairs and she couldn't see me. I spread out the drop cloth, taped off the ceiling, baseboards, and window frame and set to work.

After I finished the first coat, I decided to paint the closet. I wanted to take the closet doors off and struggled to get them off the track, but finally removed them and placed them in the hallway. This was the first time I had taken a look inside this closet and immediately noticed something strange. There was a small door in the bottom right corner of the closet wall. It was about four feet high and two feet wide. A small latch hung next to it, but it wasn't hooked. And I could see light seeping in around the edges of the miniature door.

CHAPTER SEVEN

There was no handle or knob, but I was able to use my fingers to grip the edge and pull the door open. I knelt down and peered into the space. Light poured in. I had to crouch to get through the opening, but once through I was able to stand. The room was nearly as large as the baby's room and the light came from a window. As I thought about it, there were two upstairs windows in the front of the house, but only one in the baby's room. Obviously this was the room that housed the other window.

A thick layer of dust covered the floor. "I wonder why this room doesn't have an entrance from the hallway," I said to the empty room. Did Mary know about this place? Should I ask her? The room was a good size. Was there some way I could put it to use?

I turned around and looked at the way I had come. I visualized the outside entrance having stacks of boxes against it, making it invisible.

A panic room. That's how I could use it. It wouldn't be like a real panic room—the walls weren't made of reinforced steel or anything—but it was a hidden room. A place where I could go if I felt threatened.

A place where I could hide from Trevor.

And that's really what it came down to. I wanted a place where I could go if Trevor showed up.

The paint job in the baby's room forgotten, I went downstairs and got the broom and dustpan and brought them back to the secret room. I opened the window to help with the dust I was sure to create, then carefully swept, trying to minimize the dust in the air. I had to get a trash can to dump the dust piles in, but after several passes across the wood floor, all but a thin layer of dust was gone.

Next, I got the mop and a water-filled bucket and mopped up the remaining dust.

"That's much better," I said.

The walls looked like they were off-white, but could use a wipe-down. I got fresh water in the bucket, along with a sponge, and proceeded to wipe down the walls. By the time I was done, I was soaked with sweat, but the room couldn't be any cleaner.

I wanted to bring something soft to sit or lay on, just in case I needed to actually spend time in there. The doorway was too small to bring in actual furniture, but a medium-sized bean bag chair would work.

My mental list was growing, so I decided I'd better start writing down the things I needed to buy. I put all the cleaning supplies away and then found my notepad and started a list. A knock at the door sent my heart into a gallop and I almost rushed up the stairs to hide in my panic room.

"I've got to calm down," I murmured.

Greta had started barking at the knocking. I debated whether to let her out of her crate, but decided not to.

As I approached the front door, I saw a familiar car in the driveway and felt myself relax.

"Mary," I said after I opened the door. "How are you?"

"I'm doing well. But I wanted to see how you're settling in."

"How thoughtful of you. Please come in." I closed the door behind her as she stepped into the living room.

"This color is lovely, Kate."

I smiled, feeling proud of my paint job despite the uncomfortable feeling when she used my fake name.

"This place is really shaping up." She turned to me, then she turned toward Greta's barking. "And what do we have here?"

Greta's barking began to grow more insistent. I followed Mary into the dining room where Greta was locked in her crate.

"May I let her out?" Mary asked.

I nodded and watched as Mary unlatched the crate. Greta bounded out and nearly knocked Mary over.

"Greta, no!" I scolded, embarrassed by my puppy's behavior. I was able to grab her collar and keep her from jumping on my guest.

"It's all right, Kate. She doesn't know any better. She's just a puppy." Mary leaned down and scratched Greta's chin.

"We started obedience school yesterday, but I think it will take a while for her to learn her manners."

Mary just laughed. Then she looked at me more closely. "You're awfully dusty."

I noticed a twinkle in her eyes.

"You didn't find the secret room, did you?"

She smiled when she asked, so I didn't think I had done anything wrong. "As a matter of fact, I did. When I was painting the baby's room, I found it."

"I'll bet you were surprised."

Squatting next to Greta, I looked up at Mary and nodded.

"I know exactly how you felt. Shortly after we moved in, my husband found it too. We asked our realtor about it, but all she knew was that the previous owner was a bit eccentric and had it built that way. We had intended to make it into a regular room by putting an entrance in the hallway, but by the time we needed the space, we had bought a larger house and we never got back to the project."

"Have your previous tenants asked to have it changed?"

"There have only been two other tenants before you. One was an older couple and they never mentioned it—I'm not sure they even knew about the room. And the last tenant was a single gentleman. He discovered the room, but didn't need the space, and didn't want to be bothered by any renovations. What about you, Kate? Would you like to have it converted into a regular room?"

"No," I answered, a bit too quickly. "No, it's fine. I have enough space without it. And anyway, maybe when my baby gets older he or she could use it as a play area."

"All right then." Mary glanced into the back yard. "By the way, you're welcome to plant flowers or vegetables in the yard if you'd like."

"Well, thank you," I said as I stood. "I may do that." I let go of Greta's collar, but she stayed in place.

Mary reached out and placed her hand on my arm. "I just want you to make this your home, Kate."

I could see the compassion in her eyes and felt a lump form in my throat. I nodded in response, afraid if I opened my mouth I would burst into tears.

"I'll let you get back to your painting, dear," she said, pulling her arm away.

"Thank you for everything," I managed to say.

Mary nodded and walked toward the front door. I followed behind her. She opened the door, then said, "If you need anything, you just give me a call."

"I will."

With that, she left. I locked the door behind her, then took Greta out back to let her run around for a while. I threw the ball for her, and when she was panting I led her back inside and to her pet bed and she curled up, but kept her eyes on me as I fixed myself lunch.

After I cleaned up, I wanted to keep working on the baby's room. Though I wanted to leave Greta out of her crate, I wasn't sure what she'd do—I didn't want her to be underfoot while I worked. I decided to give it a try and let her follow me up the stairs. I set her pet bed in the hallway, just outside the door, and invited her to lay down. Not surprisingly, she declined, instead going around the room, sniffing all the edges. It didn't take long for her to discover the secret room, especially since I'd left the door open.

She scampered inside and I crawled in after her. I let her get familiar with the place. After a few minutes I encouraged her to come back into the baby's room. When she did, I closed and latched the door. I got her to lay on her pet bed, but as soon as I started rolling paint on the closet wall, she became curious and trotted over to investigate.

Reluctantly, I took her back to her crate, then went upstairs and continued painting. When I had finished the inside of the closet, I decided the room would need one more coat, but it wouldn't be ready for several hours and that evening I had my first self-defense class. After I cleaned the paint brushes, I showered and changed into a pair of sweats, then had a light dinner and drove to the place where the self-defense lesson would be given.

When I walked in I saw about a dozen women plus one instructor. There were two pairs of what looked like mothers with their teenage daughters, so I wasn't the youngest one in the room. But I suspected I was the only one who was pregnant. I wasn't sure if that was something I needed to bring to the instructor's attention. Not really wanting to, I decided I would just be extra cautious.

I looked at the other women, not expecting to see any familiar faces, so it was with surprise that I recognized Billi, the woman from my dog training class. She was standing by herself so I hurried over.

"Hi there, Billi."

"Oh hey! Kate, right?"

"Yeah. What are you doing here?"

"Same thing as you, I imagine. Learning to protect myself."

"Of course," I said, feeling stupid for asking. But she hadn't answered in an unfriendly way, so I knew it was just me feeling dumb and not her trying to make me feel that way.

"It's funny to run into you here though," she said.

I nodded. "So how's Chloe doing?"

"Same as usual. Always looking for something to chew on."

A moment later the instructor had us gather around him. He looked like was in his early thirties and he introduced himself as Steve. He had blond hair and light colored eyes. In some ways he reminded me of Trevor and for a moment I missed having him around. I realized I didn't hate him—in fact I still loved him. At least I loved the man I thought I'd married. But I was afraid of him. Afraid of how he would react to random things, afraid of what he would do to me if he found me.

Pulling my thoughts away from Trevor, I focused on what Steve was saying. Before he taught us any self-defense moves, he talked about how to avoid situations where self-defense would be required. Stay alert to your surroundings, have a buddy walk with you to your car, especially after dark.

As he went over his list, I noticed he didn't mention avoiding possessive, jealous husbands. Well, I guess it's too late for that anyway, I thought.

Then he talked about how our bodies reacted to an accelerated heart rate. He explained that as our heart rate increased, our vision would narrow and our hearing would diminish. To counteract that, it was important to take a deep breath.

Finally he showed us some simple moves to break free from an assailant. He had us each try it out with him. I watched him go through the steps with each of the women. First he would come up behind a woman and wrap his arms around her, immobilizing her, then she would do a series of moves to break loose. Then he would approach the woman from the front and she would deflect his attempt to grab her, and then push him away.

Then it was my turn. I stood with my back to him, anticipating him grabbing me. Even though I was expecting it, when his arms went around me and I was immobilized, I froze. For the life of me I couldn't remember the moves I was supposed to make.

"Peel my finger back," he said into my ear.

34

Even though his words told me what to do, I wasn't able to get my body to obey.

"Come on, Kate," I heard Billi say, encouragement clear in her voice.

I looked at her and she nodded and I was finally able to respond. I peeled his pinky away from his fist, holding it with my whole hand, then pulled it backward until his hands released me.

Then he had me face him, my body in a defensive stance. As he approached me I saw Trevor's face superimposed over his, and panic engulfed me. The instructor must have seen the fear in my eyes, because he stopped short and didn't touch me. I stared at him, his face coming into focus as Trevor's face faded. Steve must have been able to tell that I had gotten control over my fear because he asked if I was ready to try it again. I nodded and he backed up a couple of steps, then walked quickly toward me. I used my arms to deflect his attempt to grab me, then used one hand to push him in the chest and force him to take a step back.

"Very good," he said.

Proud that I was able to successfully execute the moves I'd learned, I felt even happier that I had been able to push Trevor from my mind.

But what if it had actually been Trevor? All good feelings fled as I realized that a real encounter with Trevor might end up differently than my brief encounter with my instructor, which had been in a controlled environment.

I suddenly wanted to practice more. Fortunately, Steve told us to find a partner and take turns being the assailant and victim. Billi and I worked together perfecting our movements. Steve came around to each pair, correcting where needed and praising when deserved. Billi and I were doing pretty well. He only made a few suggestions to help us get it right.

At the end of class I was exhausted. I said good night to Billi and we went our separate ways.

The next morning I put the last coat of paint on the walls of the baby's room. While cleaning up, I thought about the baby. He or she was still kind of an abstract idea—I couldn't feel any movement yet and I hadn't heard the heartbeat. I knew I needed to go to a doctor for a checkup to make sure everything was proceeding normally. I had been taking over-the-counter prenatal vitamins though and trying to eat healthy, so I didn't think the doctor would tell me to do anything different.

Now that I was feeling settled in, it was time to find a doctor and make an appointment. I guessed I was about ten weeks along, so I knew I should go to a doctor soon.

As I stood at the kitchen sink patting the paint brush dry on a paper towel, I gazed out the window into the backyard. Mary had told me I could plant flowers or vegetables. I had done a little gardening with Dad and had enjoyed the result. I decided I'd buy some plants and beautify the yard.

I had let Greta out of her crate before I started washing out the paint brushes and now she was jumping on my leg, trying to get my attention. As I looked down at her, I wondered if she would destroy anything I planted. I decided I would figure that out later.

I took Greta out back to play for a while, then I put her in the crate before driving to a local plant nursery. Walking up and down the rows of flowers, I enjoyed the process of selecting colorful flowers that pleased me. I bought some hand tools to help me with the job, then took my purchases home.

I had lived in the house less than a week, but was quickly beginning to feel at home there. I still had several things I wanted to do to make it my own, but I felt good about all that I had accomplished so far.

Opening the side gate, I made several trips to bring all of my purchases into the backyard. Once done, I latched the gate and went into the house so I could let Greta into the backyard while I worked.

She pranced around, anxious to have me toss the ball for her. I threw it a few times, then set it at my feet.

"I'm going to plant these flowers now, girl. You're going to have to keep yourself entertained for a while."

She picked the ball up and looked in my direction, a hopeful look in her eyes. I felt bad ignoring her—she had been my constant companion since I'd gotten her—but she needed to learn that sometimes I had other things to do.

I walked around the large yard, Greta trotting along next to me, trying to decide where I wanted to plant the various flowers. I had bought a mixture of annuals and perennials and wanted to spread them around the yard in a somewhat organized fashion.

Next, I placed the pots in the places where I wanted to plant them. Standing on the back porch, I looked at the effect. After making a few adjustments, I felt ready to begin.

So far Greta hadn't bothered any of the plants, but then I hadn't started digging yet. Sure enough, as I dug a fresh hole in the rich soil, Greta poked her nose in and began sniffing furiously. I pushed her away and set the first flower in the hole, then filled the hole with dirt and patted it in place.

As I moved to the next plant, Greta continued to investigate the first one.

"Greta, come!" I commanded, but she ignored me, not at all trained yet.

I kept an eye on her as I planted a few more flowers. Though interested in the plants, she hadn't tried to dig any up yet. Unexpectedly, her attention zeroed in on the gate that led to the front yard, and then she began barking.

The blood drained from my face and my eyes were riveted to the gate. It was too high for me to see who was there and I expected Trevor to come barging through in seconds. But when I heard a female voice, relief cascaded over me.

"Yoo hoo. Is anyone home?" the voice called.

I had been kneeling and pushed myself to a standing position. I walked toward the gate, wondering who it was. It didn't sound like Mary's voice. Undoing the gate latch, I pulled the door open and saw a woman holding a plate of cookies. She appeared to be in her late forties. Her hair was brown and cut in a short style. Friendliness was clear on her face.

"Hello," I said.

"You must be Kate."

"Yes, I am." I was alarmed that this stranger knew who I was and where I lived.

"I'm Trish. I live next door." She pointed off to the right where a house stood about a hundred yards away.

"Oh," I said. "It's nice to meet you. Would you like to sit down?"

"Sure." She held the plate of cookies out to me. "These are for you. I hope you like chocolate chip."

I took the plate. "Thank you. They're my favorite."

"Wonderful."

I led her to the back porch. Greta had stopped barking but was trying to catalog the woman's scent. I shoved Greta away and invited Trish to sit with me on the steps of the back porch. "I'm sorry. I don't have any chairs back here yet."

"That's all right," she said, sitting on the step near me.

Still concerned that she'd known my name, I asked, "How did you know my name is Kate?"

She laughed and it was the kind of laugh that made you want to laugh along. "Mary told me all about you. I think she's developed a soft spot for you. You probably remind her of her granddaughters. They live back East and she doesn't get to see them very often."

Her explanation made me feel much better, although I hoped Mary wasn't telling all of her friends about me. Suddenly I was very glad I'd told her my name was Kate.

"She's been very kind to me," I said.

"Where did you move from?"

This was not a question I had planned for. In fact, I hadn't even thought of the story I would tell if someone were to ask how I became widowed. "Las Vegas," I blurted out, not knowing where that came from. It made sense though. My license plates said Nevada, I didn't want to tell anyone I had moved from Reno, and Vegas was large enough that no one there would be expected to know me.

"So you're used to the heat then."

"Yes," I lied. In fact, I'd never lived anyplace where it got as hot as it did in Vegas.

"Our summers won't seem so bad then."

"How hot does it get here in the summer?" I asked, now worried that I might be miserable.

"Most days are in the nineties, but a couple of weeks are over one hundred. But it's more humid here than Vegas. That's where you might notice the difference."

I nodded, contemplating how it was going to feel to be pregnant in that heat. My attention was drawn to Greta, who had started digging around one of the newly planted flowers. I jumped up and ran to her. "Greta, no!" I grabbed her collar and pulled her away. Shaking my finger in her face I said, "No!"

She whined, knowing she had done something to displease me. I brought her back to the porch steps, holding on to her collar with one hand and petting her with the other.

Trish laughed. "She's a bit of a handful, huh?"

I laughed too. "Yeah, but she's a good dog. She's going to obedience school, so I have high hopes."

"Did you know you can put chili pepper powder around your plants to repel the dog?"

"Oh. I didn't know that. I'll have to give that a try."

"Well, Kate, I'll let you get back to your planting," Trish said, standing.

I had to hold tight to Greta's collar. When Trish stood, Greta jerked forward, trying to get loose. "Thank you for the cookies."

I finally let Greta go and she excitedly sniffed Trish. I pushed Greta away and walked with Trish to the gate.

Trish stopped and turned toward me. "If you need anything, you just come on over." She smiled warmly. "I mean it."

I smiled back, touched by her sincerity. "I will." I latched the gate behind her, then went back to planting flowers. I worked until I had planted each one. Standing back to admire my work, I smiled, loving the beauty the flowers added to the yard.

Chapter Eight

The next week I drove to my first appointment with the obstetrician. I had found the doctor's name when I did a search for local female OB's. When I checked in, they asked me to pay for the appointment up front since I didn't have insurance. But they also gave me a discount since they wouldn't have to deal with an insurance company. I paid in cash so they wouldn't have to see my real name.

The nurse weighed me—I had gained five pounds—then took my blood pressure, which was normal, and placed me in a room. I sat on a chair in the corner. Doctor Eggleston came in a short time later. When she asked me questions about my health, I had no trouble answering. But when she began asking about the baby's father, I became nervous. Even though as my doctor she was supposed to keep our conversation confidential, I felt certain that she would have to write it down somewhere. I had just met her and didn't want to divulge all my secrets just yet. I had removed my wedding ring, not wanting to show there may be a man in my life.

"The baby's father is out of the picture," I said, saying the words I had mentally rehearsed.

"I see," she said. "Who do you have as your support?"

I must have looked confused because she said, "For example, who will be with you in the delivery room?"

I felt tears sting my eyes and I hated myself for getting emotional so easily. I bit the inside of my lip to distract myself, then blinked a few times to clear my eyes. Dr. Eggleston watched me and I felt extremely self-conscious. I thought about the people in my life and found the list tragically short. Finally I said, "I, uh, I haven't decided yet."

Dr. Eggleston smiled at me, apparently used to pregnant women who became emotional. "Well, you have a while to decide."

I smiled back, relieved the hard questions were over.

Dr. Eggleston stood and patted the exam table. "Let's get a look at your baby, shall we?"

I grinned, thrilled to get to the part of the appointment I had been looking forward to. I climbed onto the table and lay back. Dr. Eggleston pulled up by blouse, exposing my still flat stomach. She squirted gel onto my belly, then pressed a device against my abdomen. Immediately the room filled with the sound of a strong, rapid heartbeat.

Tears filled my eyes, but this time I didn't care. Dr. Eggleston turned the monitor in my direction and I saw a blob on the screen, dancing and jumping around.

"Your baby is certainly active," she said.

Suddenly worried, I said, "Is that normal?"

"Oh yes. Perfectly normal."

I smiled, reassured. "Can you tell if it's a boy or a girl?"

"No, it's too soon. You'll have another ultrasound at twenty weeks. You'll be able to find out then."

I nodded.

She lifted the device from my belly and the room went silent. She wiped the gel off with a paper cloth. "I'd like to see you again in six weeks."

I sat up. "Okay."

She handed me a snapshot of the ultrasound image. "Your first baby picture."

Staring at the image, I smiled. "Thank you."

On my way out I made the follow-up appointment, then walked to my car. The baby seemed real now. Not just an abstract idea, but a tiny, very real human being. An image of the baby's room filled my mind and all I saw was an empty green room. I had absolutely nothing for the baby yet.

Pulling out of the doctor's parking lot, I drove toward the Wal-Mart. Though I would be happy with second-hand furniture, I remembered reading that when it came to cribs, it was better to buy new. Some of the older cribs were unsafe and I wasn't about to take a chance with my baby's safety.

There were several cribs to choose from. After deliberating for a while I made my selection. I had to have an employee help me load the box into my car. He slid it onto the floor in front of the back seats. I drove home, excited to get the crib set up.

Once I got home I realized I had a problem. I had been so excited to get the crib that I hadn't thought through how I was going to get it into the house or how I was going to put it together.

I remembered Trish's visit the previous week and her sincere offer to come over if I needed anything.

Maybe when her husband comes home he can help me, I thought.

The day was sunny but not too warm so I decided to walk to Trish's house. First I put my purse in the house, then said hello to Greta. On impulse, I took out Greta's leash, deciding to bring her along. She pranced around, ecstatic to see me and to be let out of her crate.

I locked the front door behind me and dropped the key in my jeans pocket, then set out for Trish's house. It took ten minutes to walk there, mostly because Greta kept stopping to either mark her territory or to investigate bugs and other smells.

Finally I turned up the paved driveway to Trish's house. Her house was much larger than my little cottage and the yard was beautifully manicured. As I approached the door, it suddenly occurred to me that she might not know I was pregnant. I really had no idea what Mary had told her about me. How was I going to explain what I needed?

Well, my pregnancy will be apparent soon enough, I thought. No reason to hide the truth about that at least.

I rang the doorbell, trying to figure out how I was going to phrase my request. I was so preoccupied with my thoughts, I didn't hear anyone coming to the door. Unexpectedly, it opened. I opened my mouth, ready to explain to Trish what I needed, but I was swiftly silenced when I saw who had opened the door.

CHAPTER NINE

A man, a few years older than me, stood on the threshold. He had the most gorgeous green eyes I had ever seen. I wondered if it was his natural color or if he was wearing colored contacts. His dark hair was so short as to be nearly shaved. Muscles bulged against the sleeves of his t-shirt.

"Can I help you?" he asked, smiling.

As I gazed at his handsome face, I had nearly forgotten why I had come over. Greta tugged against her leash, wanting to check out the new human.

"Marcus, who's at the door?" a woman's voice called.

Marcus turned toward the woman, who stepped into the doorway.

"Kate," Trish said. "Hello."

When I saw Trish, I finally found my voice. "Hi."

"Marcus, this is our new neighbor, Kate."

He gave a curt nod in my direction.

"Kate, this is my son, Marcus."

"Hi," I said again, captivated by his eyes.

"He's in the marines and just got home today. We hadn't been expecting him for a while so it was a wonderful surprise." She put her arm around his waist, the top of her head just reaching his shoulder. "And we're so glad he's back."

When Trish had come over to introduce herself and she and I had chatted, we'd never gotten to the part where she had a handsome son.

"What brings you over, Kate?" Trish asked.

Suddenly realizing I was interrupting a family reunion, I didn't want to tell her why I'd come. "It's nothing. It can wait."

"Nonsense," she said in a friendly way. "You obviously came here for a reason. Now what was it?"

Feeling awkward, I tried to make light of what I needed. "Well, it's just that I bought something and I needed some help carrying it into the house. But it can wait. I was going to see if your husband could help me when he has some time."

"Jeff is actually out of town for the next week, but Marcus can help you, right son?"

"Yes, ma'am," he said, smiling.

For some reason, I was reluctant to accept his offer of help. It's true that I found him attractive, but I had zero interest in getting involved with anyone. Plus, there was the minor fact that I was still married.

But what does any of that have to do with allowing him to help me bring in the crib, I thought.

I was confused and didn't understand my feelings. But I did know I couldn't drag the crib into the house by myself and it was highly unlikely that I could put it together myself either. Trish and Marcus were looking at me, waiting for my answer. "That would be great. Thanks."

Marcus stepped onto the porch, putting Greta into a frenzy. She jumped against his leg, trying to get a good sniff. I pulled on her leash. "Greta, no!" As usual, she ignored me, but fortunately I was still stronger than her and was able to pull her back.

Marcus knelt down and let her smell his hand. "Is that better?" he asked her. She happily licked his hand, apparently accepting him.

"Nice dog," he said, looking up at me.

"Thanks. I just got her last week."

He nodded, then stood. "You ready to get started?"

I really wasn't. I would have preferred someone safe, like Trish's husband, but it didn't seem I had a choice at this point. "Sure." I started walking down the driveway and he fell into step beside me. He was about a head taller than me, I noticed.

"So, what's this thing you need help bringing in your house?"

It was a good thing I was looking in front of me. If Marcus had seen my face, I'm sure I would have looked like a deer caught in the proverbial headlights. Since he had just gotten home, I seriously doubted Trish had told him anything about me. Plus I didn't know if she was even aware of my pregnancy. "You'll see," I hedged.

He laughed. "Okay."

We had to stop a few times as Greta paused. It seemed there was no forcing her to move if she didn't want to.

"So, your mom said you just got home," I started, trying to be friendly. "Where were you before?"

"I've been stationed in Afghanistan for the last two years."

"Oh. How was it there?" Out of the corner of my eye I saw him look at me.

"It's pretty rough over there. It's nice to be home."

I glanced at him and nodded.

We finally reached the gravel drive that led to my house, and turned up the road. In moments we stood next to my car. I pointed to the large box in the back seat.

"So this is the mystery item," he said, reaching for the door. He pulled it open and grabbed the box, sliding it out the door. Once it was out of the car and sitting on the driveway, the word 'crib' was plainly visible.

I saw him look at it, but he made no comment.

"Where would you like it?"

"I'll show you." I walked to the front door, fished the key out of my pocket, and turned the lock. I held the door open for him as he easily carried the box into the living room. I closed the door and pointed to the stairs. "This way." He followed me up the stairs and into the baby's room. "You can just set it over there," I said, pointing to a wall.

He set it down, careful to not damage the wall. "Smells like you painted recently."

"Yes." I had never been very good at small talk and this was no exception.

"Do you need help with anything else?"

I really wanted to ask him to put the crib together, but I knew I wouldn't need it for months and I wasn't ready to explain my situation. Maybe I could have Trish's husband Jeff do it when he got back from his business trip. "No, I think that will do it. Thanks for your help."

"Yes, ma'am." He headed out the bedroom door and down the stairs.

When he opened the front door, he paused and turned toward me. I noticed his eyes flicker to my stomach, but I knew it was impossible to tell I was pregnant just by looking. I looked at him, waiting for him to say what was on his mind.

"Never mind." He shook his head. "Take care," he said instead.

"You too." I locked the door behind him, then went to the front window and watched him walk toward the street that ran in front of our houses.

I pulled out my laptop and brought up my email account. I had been checking my emails daily. Trevor had sent a few more emails, each getting progressively angrier, but I had resisted the urge to respond. I'd also been checking the Reno newspaper every day to watch for any information about Trevor's arrest. So far there had been no mention of anything and I wondered if the charges had been dropped or a plea deal made.

Alyssa, my friend from Reno, had emailed me back, but she was still at her parents' house. Though I really wanted to give her all the details of my new life, I hadn't told her where I'd moved, only that I had left. It saddened me that I couldn't tell my friend more. Alyssa was the only person I really had a connection with who knew the truth about my life.

As I thought about my safety I wondered if it might be best if I were to just reinvent myself and put my past behind me. I knew I couldn't cut Alyssa out completely, but I had to minimize my contact. I had to think of my safety and the safety of my baby.

The first thing I wanted to do was sell Dad's house. The idea had been hovering in the back of my mind for the last couple of weeks, but now it had pushed itself forward and I knew it was best. That night was Greta's second dog obedience class and the next night I had my second self-defense class. I would leave early in the morning the day after my class.

Chapter Ten

I went to Greta's obedience class that night and learned some techniques to use with her. Billi was there with Chloe. We were both busy with our dogs and didn't have a chance to do more than say hello. The next night I went to my second self-defense lesson. This time when Steve had me practice what I'd been taught, I responded with confidence. Throughout the previous week I'd practiced some of the movements and also visualized myself using them, which seemed to help.

Early the following morning I loaded a suitcase with the items I thought I'd need, filled a container of dog food, grabbed Greta's pet bed, then strapped Greta into the passenger seat with the special doggie seatbelt I'd bought. She didn't seem to mind being restrained and this way she wouldn't get in my way while I drove or get hurt if I had to stop suddenly.

It took half the day to reach Reno, mostly because I had to stop a few times to give Greta breaks. As we passed through Reno I thought about Trevor and wondered what he was doing. Though I knew it was unlikely Trevor would see me, I couldn't help but watch the cars around me, fearful that he would somehow know I was in town and find me.

I pushed him out of my mind and drove on to Lovelock. When I arrived at my house I was ready for a break and happy to have gotten there. Everything looked as I remembered it. I took Greta inside and she went to work thoroughly exploring. I brought in our belongings and sat on the couch. A plume of dust filled the air, making me cough.

As I looked around, I could see it would be a big job to get the place ready to sell. I had left minimal utilities on—I hadn't wanted the pipes to freeze—but there was no Internet access here. I found the phone book and searched for a cleaning service. Using my cell phone, I arranged to have someone come out the next afternoon and do a thorough cleaning.

My next task was to decide what to do with the furniture and Dad's belongings. Fortunately I had already packed up most of the house in the few months between Dad's passing and me heading off to the University in Reno. Walking around the house and looking at the furniture, I realized it was mostly old and not in the best condition. Money had been tight and decorating the house hadn't been high on Dad's priority list.

I thought about Mary and her generosity in giving me the furniture that was now in my house. I thought it might be nice if I could do the same for someone else. Grabbing the yellow pages again, I looked up a charity that advertised their willingness to pick up goods. When I called, they said they had a cancellation and could come by the next morning. I hoped they would be gone in time for the cleaning people to come over.

With a notepad and pen in hand, I walked to each room, writing down which pieces of furniture to donate and which to have shipped to my place in California. By the time I was done, there were very few items I wanted to keep. I had decided to keep the new television, some linens, and all of the photos.

Next I went out to the garage, where I had stored all the boxes I'd packed up the previous summer. I had been careful to label each box. I divided the boxes into two groups—those that I would keep and those that I would donate. Since I had very little storage space at my California house, I wanted to minimize my "keep" pile.

After working for thirty minutes, I looked over at Greta, who had curled up in a corner of the garage, and smiled. She had been very good while I had worked and I was pleased. Deciding to take a break and reward her, I brought her out back and threw the ball for a while. Then I gave her a good scratch and she seemed to smile with pleasure.

Hunger pangs reminded me it was time for lunch, but there was no food in the house. I needed to go to the grocery store and buy enough food to sustain me for the few days I'd be here. Debating whether to trust Greta to be left on her own in the house or to take her with me and leave her in the car, I decided to leave her home. I hoped that our little play time had tired her out enough that she would behave. I had brought her pet bed into the house, so I encouraged her to lay on it, then grabbing my purse, I went out the door.

Within thirty minutes I was back and found Greta waiting for my return. It didn't appear that she had bothered anything. When she saw me, she ran over for some attention. "You're a good girl," I said, scratching between her ears. Her tail wagged happily.

After fixing myself lunch, I took the food out back and let Greta spend some time outside while I ate. Fifteen minutes later I called to Greta, "Okay, girl, time to get back to work." When I opened the door she raced to be the first inside and I patted her as she pushed past me.

I spent the next two hours finalizing my decisions on whether each item in the house would stay or go. By the time all was said and done, I had very little that I wanted to keep. I realized that the things I really wanted were at my apartment in Reno. Things like the kitchen implements that had belonged to my Dad. But I especially wanted my Christmas ornaments. Each one had a special memory associated with it. But they were in Trevor's possession now.

I wanted them back.

Chapter Eleven

The truck arrived first thing the next morning. I showed the men which items and boxes I wanted to donate and they had them loaded in less than an hour. After they left I walked around the house and couldn't believe how empty it was. The house just didn't feel like the same place where I had spent so much time with Dad.

I gathered all the items I wanted to keep into a corner of the living room and fixed myself some lunch. I had decided to leave the refrigerator for whoever bought the house. When I'd gone to the store I'd bought a package of disposable plates and utensils so that I could prepare simple meals without using dishes.

As I ate, I thought about the best way to get the items I was keeping to my new place in California. I knew I couldn't fit everything in my Honda, so I decided to spend the money to have it all shipped. Because there wasn't a lot, I hoped the cost would be relatively low. I had kept the yellow pages and found a listing for shipping companies. After calling a few, I found one whose prices were reasonable and I arranged to have them come by the next day to pick up my stuff.

That afternoon the cleaning crew came and spent several hours making the place spotless. I paid them and thanked them for doing such a great job. I thought the walls could use a coat of paint, but decided to put the house on the market as is and see what happened. As I was looking at the now familiar yellow pages for realtors, I ran across an ad for an agent whose name looked familiar. Then I remembered he'd been a friend of Dad's. I called him and explained who I was and what I wanted to do. He promised to come over as soon as he had a free minute.

A little while later Don Hunter knocked on my door. I put Greta in the backyard so she wouldn't get in the way and invited Dad's old friend in.

"Hi, Lily," he said. "How are you?"

It felt strange to hear someone call me Lily. I had started getting used to going by Kate. "I'm doing fine. Like I said on the phone, I've decided to sell Dad's house. Would you be interested in listing it?"

"Absolutely."

We discussed the details and set a price, then I signed the paperwork making him my real estate agent. He promised to get the house listed the next day and I gave him my cell number so he could keep me informed.

That night I slept on a sleeping bag I had kept—I had donated my mattress since I already had a bed in California that worked fine—and woke up feeling stiff. Greta had curled up next to me, once again keeping me company and helping me to not feel alone.

The shipping company came later that morning and took care of the items I wanted shipped. Once they had left, there was no reason for me to stay. I packed my suitcase and loaded Greta and our things into my Honda. Before leaving, I went inside one last time and mentally said good-bye. I still had my memories and felt good about putting Lovelock behind me.

It took less than two hours to reach Reno. The more I thought about the belongings in Trevor's possession, the more determined I became to retrieve them. I wondered if my key to the apartment would still work. I had only been gone a few weeks, so it was possible that Trevor hadn't bothered to change the locks. Technically, the lease for the apartment was under my name, so I had every right to go in and take what belonged to me. The biggest challenge would be doing it without Trevor knowing.

As I entered the outer edges of Reno, I wondered if I should just keep going and forget about getting my belongings back. The thought of running into Trevor nearly paralyzed me. What would he do if he caught me? Would he try to imprison me again? Would I be able to get away? Should I even risk it? It was only stuff anyway. Was it really that important?

When I imagined the upcoming Christmas and pictured my Christmas tree with nothing but store bought ornaments, and imagined my treasured ornaments either displayed on Trevor's tree, or left in the closet, or worse yet, destroyed, fury overtook my paralysis and I knew I had to at least try to get my belongings. They were meaningless to Trevor but meant everything to me. It just wasn't right that he should have them.

I decided I would start by driving past Rob's Auto Body shop. That's where Trevor had been working when I'd left a few weeks ago. It didn't take long to get there and I drove slowly by. My purpose in going was to see if Trevor's car was parked there. If it was, I would feel pretty safe in going to the apartment and getting my things. But as soon as the shop came into view, it was clear that something was wrong. The large doors for the car bays were all closed and there were no cars in the parking lot. It looked like Rob's Auto Body shop was closed.

Driving past, I continued on for a few minutes, then pulled into a parking lot and turned off my car, wondering what to do next. Greta looked at me expectantly, so I reached over and patted her. She stood on the seat and began wagging her tail, but the doggie seatbelt kept her from moving around too much. I thought it might be a good idea to go somewhere where she could get out for a few minutes and I could think about my next move. Since I had recently moved from the area, I was familiar with the location of the parks and we drove to the nearest one.

After attaching Greta's leash to her collar, I helped her out of the car and we walked around the edges of the park. When she stopped to explore a particularly interesting bush, I pulled out my cell phone and called information to get the number for Rob's Auto Body shop. The operator gave me the number and asked if I wanted to be connected. I said yes and listened to the phone ring. After several rings a recording came on and said the number had been disconnected.

Wow, I thought. I guess they've gone out of business. This information added a new twist to my plans. If Trevor no longer worked there, where did he work? And if he was unemployed, had an arrest hanging over him, and was most likely broke, how would he feel if he saw me? Would he blame me for all of his problems? Would he get violent?

Chapter Twelve

I drove toward my old apartment with caution. Even as I approached the place where I used to live, I could easily see Trevor's blue Camaro parked at the curb. I knew if he were to see my Honda he would recognize it. Pulling to the side of the road half a dozen houses away, I hoped that from this distance he wouldn't notice me.

After half an hour with nothing happening, I started thinking about ways to draw Trevor away from the apartment. Then it came to me. I could call him and ask him to meet me somewhere. Somewhere far enough away to give me time to go in, get my stuff, and get out. And I had to have enough time to do this before he realized I was a no show.

As I contemplated speaking to him, I could feel myself getting shaky. I was afraid how he would respond to me calling him and I wasn't so sure he'd even be interested or willing to meet me. I thought about the emails he'd sent and how he'd threatened me.

Is this really worth it? Just to get back some ornaments? It seemed silly as I thought about it, but deep down I felt like I needed to prove to myself that I could take control of my life and that I had every right to retrieve my personal belongings.

Taking a deep breath, I first pressed star sixty-seven so that my number would be hidden from Trevor's caller ID. Then I punched in his number from memory. I listened as it rang once, twice, then I heard his familiar voice.

"Hello?"

My heart raced and I felt my hands go clammy.

"Hello?" he asked again.

My lips moved, but no sound came out.

"I can hear you breathing." He paused, then demanded, "Who is this?"

"Trevor?" It came out as a whisper and I had to clear my throat. "Trevor," I said more loudly.

He was silent, then said, "Lily? Is that you?"

I could picture the look of uncertainty on his face. "Yes." I said it with more confidence than I felt.

"Where are you?"

My eyes were glued to the apartment, half-expecting him to come running out and see me. I realized I had one hand poised above the key in the ignition, ready to bolt at the slightest movement. I heard Greta panting next to me and somehow looking at her gave me courage. "I'm here. In Reno."

I could hear him gasp.

"Where exactly? Can I see you?"

I hadn't expected him to take the bait quite so easily and I found myself smiling. *This is going to be easier than I thought.* I decided to play it coy. "I *would* like to meet with you, but I'm scared."

"You don't need to be scared, Lily. I won't do anything to hurt you. I promise." He paused. "I love you."

His voice cracked and I thought he might be crying. I started to feel guilty for tricking him. He would be excited to see me and then I wouldn't show up. Imagining how I would feel in his place, I felt my resolve slipping. I took a deep breath, trying to harden my determination. "Okay," I said. "Go to Circus Circus and wait by the midway. I'll be watching for you."

"Okay. What's your phone number? In case I need to call you."

"Trevor, I don't feel comfortable giving that to you yet. Let's see how our meeting goes first."

"Fine," he said, obviously unhappy.

I noticed his tears seemed to have stopped. Testing him, I murmured, "Maybe we shouldn't do this."

"Please, Lily. I really want to see you."

Acting like he had persuaded me, I said, "All right. I'll see you when you get here."

"I love you," he said before hanging up.

I closed my phone and stared in the direction of the apartment. It only took moments before he appeared. As I watched him walk away from the apartment and toward his car, I felt my heart pound. That man was my husband. We were in love only a few months ago. We've created the child growing in my belly. What happened to kill that love? And was it really dead?

I felt my hand reaching toward the door, ready to open it. I could feel his strong arms around me and re-experienced the happy memories we had shared. I suddenly wanted that again. I wanted it so bad that I could almost taste it. The scent of Trevor's cologne seemed to fill my nostrils and I felt such an overwhelming longing that I almost couldn't stand it.

I pulled on the door handle and the door swung open. My feet touched the pavement and I pulled myself to a standing position. I opened my mouth.

"Trevor!"

A figure approached Trevor from the direction of the apartment.

"Trevor!" the voice called again.

He turned toward the person calling out to him. I squinted, trying to identify the person who was now handing him something. I watched as Trevor leaned toward the person, then put his arms around her—I was certain now that it was a woman—and pulled her against him. It felt like someone had knocked the wind out of me. Then, when he pressed his mouth to hers, I heard myself actually cry out. I whipped my head back and forth to see if anyone had heard me, but it hadn't been as loud as I'd thought.

I sunk back into the car and closed the door, my eyes riveted to Trevor and the woman. They pulled apart and a memory filled my mind.

I felt myself transported back to my Sociology class. Jealousy stung my heart as I watched Trevor and a beautiful auburn-haired girl flirting.

The girl kissing Trevor was that girl. It was Amanda.

Chapter Thirteen

Why would Trevor tell me he loves me and in the next moment be kissing Amanda? Did he say "I love you" in front of her? My earlier guilt at tricking him vanished. Instead it was replaced by fury. He was the one tricking me. He didn't love me. Why would he even want to meet with me? What was his motive?

Putting that aside for the moment, I focused on my current obstacle. Trevor was pulling away from the curb, which gave me about forty minutes, but Amanda was now in the apartment. I couldn't very well go over there and barge in and demand my stuff back.

My shoulders slumped as I realized my plan had failed. It was unlikely that Trevor would fall for my ploy again. "I guess I'll just have to forget about my stuff," I said to Greta. She barked in response.

But as I thought about Trevor and Amanda living in the apartment *I* had leased, using *my* things, I felt enraged. I stared at the place where only moments before Trevor and Amanda had embraced. I was hurt that Trevor had moved on so quickly. But if he had moved on, why was he so anxious to see me? What did he want from me? Did he think he was going to take my money again? Or worse yet, did he think he was going to take my baby?

Automatically, my hands went to my abdomen in a gesture of protection. There was no way I would let that happens.

I glanced at my watch. The clock was ticking. Five minutes had passed and I had accomplished nothing. Should I confront Amanda or should I just drive away and forget the whole thing? Uncertain what to do, I looked at Greta. "What should I do, girl?" She just smiled at me with her sweet doggie smile. I reached over and pet her, then looked back toward the apartment.

My hand froze in mid-scratch as I watched Amanda walk across the grass and toward a car parked on the street. She climbed into the driver's side and a moment later she drove away. I couldn't believe it—my opportunity had come.

As soon as her car was out of sight, I drove my car forward and parked right in front of the apartment. I considered taking Greta in with me, but didn't want to take the extra time to undo her seatbelt and then have to strap her back in.

I left my purse in the car and just brought my car key and the key I had kept from the apartment. Locking my car, I raced to the apartment door and inserted the key into the lock. It worked. Grinning in relief, I pushed the door open. Memories assaulted me—both good and bad. Yes, things had gone sour with Trevor at the end, but before that we'd shared good times.

My gaze darted around the room and I saw that the place looked pretty much the same. Amanda, if she was living there, kept the place tidy. Leaving the front door open, I went into the bedroom and then stopped. The bed was unmade and I couldn't help but wonder if Trevor was sleeping with Amanda. The thought of him with another woman hurt. Even though I'd left him, we were still married. I wondered if that meant anything to him.

Pushing those troubling thoughts aside, I went to the closet and slid open the door. To my surprise, my boxes of Christmas decoration were untouched. I pulled them out and quickly carried them out to my car, placing them in the trunk. I closed the trunk and went back inside.

I looked around to see if there was anything else of mine that I wanted to take. First I searched the bedroom but nothing else of mine was there. I also noticed that none of the clothes in the closet and dresser belonged to a woman. Somehow I felt better in knowing that

Trevor appeared to live there alone.

The only other room that might contain items I'd want to take was the kitchen. I had brought a number of kitchen implements, like small appliances and mixing bowls, from Dad's house after I'd first moved in. Quickly going through the cupboards, it didn't take long for me to gather the things I wanted to take. Things like my Dad's toaster, blender and can opener as well as mixing bowls and utensils. I could use those things at my new place in California. And, after all, they were mine. There was no reason I should have to go out and buy new things when I had these.

Glancing at my watch, I knew Trevor had been gone about twenty minutes and Amanda about fifteen. Time was getting short, but I thought I could get it done. When I had looked in the closet earlier, I had noticed a plastic tub that I could use to carry things out to my car.

Dashing to the closet, I dumped out the contents of the tub, which looked like some gaming equipment of Trevor's. Then I took the tub to the kitchen and set as much as I could fit into it, then carried the tub to my car. I opened the door behind the driver's and moved the items from the tub to the floor of the car. Greta watched my every move, but stayed in her seat, restrained by her seatbelt.

I went back into the apartment for another trip. After another trip I came back inside once more and was able to fit the remaining items, including the silverware, into the tub. I looked through the cupboards and drawers one last time to make sure I hadn't missed anything. Satisfied that I'd gotten everything that belonged to me, I took the last load out to the car and unloaded it all into the back seat.

After locking the car, I took the empty tub back into the bedroom. I was putting Trevor's gaming stuff back into the tub when an angry voice filled the room.

"What the hell are you doing?"

My head whipped up to see Amanda standing in the doorway. I sincerely hoped Trevor wasn't with her. I looked at my watch and knew

I had only minutes until he would be back. I had to get out of there. I jumped up, the tub forgotten. "I was just leaving."

"How did you get in here?"

Angry to be questioned by this girl who was in *my* apartment, I said, "Not that it's any of your business, but this is *my* apartment. The lease is in *my* name."

Clearly not convinced, Amanda shook her head. "But you don't live here anymore."

"Do you?" I shot back.

"Not yet," she said, a mean glint in her eye.

"Well, I hope you and Trevor will be very happy together." I paused. "Has he hit you yet or is he still playing the part of Prince Charming?"

She shook her head. "You don't know what you're talking about."

I knew I needed to get out of there but she stood between me and the exit. I watched as she pulled out her cell phone and pressed two buttons.

"Trevor doesn't love you anymore, Lily. You just need to get over it." Then she put the phone to her ear.

Her words sank into my heart and I felt hot tears welling up in my eyes. Even though I'd left *him*, I still loved him in a way and it cut me deeply to think he didn't love me at all.

"She's here," Amanda said into the phone. Then, "Okay." And she hung up. "Trevor wants to talk to you."

My mind spun as I focused on what Amanda had said. *Trevor was on his way. He knew I was here. I had to get away.* Gathering my wits, I shook my head. "I have nothing to say to him." Then I walked toward her. She didn't move. "Get out of my way," I demanded.

"No. Trevor told me to keep you here until he gets back."

I tried to push past her but she wrapped her arms around me. It was just like Steve, my self-defense instructor, had done. For a full second I was immobilized as I tried to recall the moves I'd practiced.

Then in a rush they came to my mind and I executed the moves exactly as Steve had taught me. Amanda cried out as I bent her finger back as hard as I could. A moment later I was free. Momentarily stunned to discover the moves really worked, it took me half a second to react. Then I raced out the door, unlocked my car with shaky hands, started the engine and drove away.

Just as I began turning the corner, I looked in my rear view mirror and saw Trevor's Camaro entering the street at the other end. I drove as fast as I dared, the adrenaline pulsing through my veins. Soon I was back on I-80 and heading west.

"Woo hoo!" I shouted, startling Greta. "I did it!" Giddy with relief, I laughed as I pictured Trevor and Amanda's faces when they realized I had cleaned out the kitchen cupboards. I hadn't taken anything that belonged to Trevor and felt no remorse for what I'd done.

As I replayed the encounter with Amanda, I felt elated. I had broken out of her grip and I had gotten away. As I continued heading west I kept a close eye on my mirrors, watching for Trevor's Camaro. As I reached Sacramento I felt safe.

I had done it.

CHAPTER FOURTEEN

Within a few hours I pulled into my driveway, exhausted. It had been quite a day. I let Greta out of the car and she stayed near me as I walked to the front door and unlocked it. The sun was starting to set and I wanted to get everything into the house before it was full dark.

There were no street lamps on my street and the porch light wouldn't penetrate the darkness near my car. I carried in the boxes with the Christmas decorations first, stacking them in the living room, then I went back out the door to get another load. As I stepped off the porch I saw a tall man jogging toward me up the gravel drive. There was just enough light for me to recognize my neighbor, Marcus.

"Hi, Kate," he said when he reached me.

I noticed he was wearing shorts and a t-shirt. "Hi," I said, wondering why he'd come over.

"I was coming back from my run and saw you carrying things in. Do you need any help?"

I was so exhausted that I was happy to have the help. "Sure. That would be nice." I had left the trunk open and pointed in that direction. "If you can get the things in the trunk, that would really help." I watched him lift my suitcase from the trunk, as well as Greta's food and then carry them into the house. I opened the door to the backseat and grabbed as many items as I could hold, and carried them into the kitchen.

"Where do you want me to put these?" he asked.

"Just on the floor in the living room is fine."

69

It didn't take long for him to bring in everything from the trunk. When he brought in his first load from the backseat and set the items on the dining room table he asked, "Where did you get all this stuff?"

The question caught me off guard. I didn't want to tell him that I'd tricked my estranged husband into leaving so that I could get into my old apartment and "steal" back my stuff. "Garage sales," I said instead, smiling.

He believed me without question and helped me bring it all in. When we'd finished, we stood in the kitchen and in the bright light I got a good look at him. In his running shorts and snug fitting t-shirt I couldn't help but notice what good shape he was in. He was all male and his nearness made my pulse quicken. But I had zero desire to get involved with anyone.

Besides, I thought, what makes you think he'd want to get involved with you? You're married *and* pregnant.

"Thanks for your help, Marcus."

"Anytime." He paused. "If you want, I can put that crib together."

I felt my face redden, like I had done something wrong. "What makes you think it's for me?"

The question seemed to embarrass him. "I'm sorry. It's none of my business."

Now I felt bad. "No, it's okay. Did your mom tell you I'm pregnant?"

He seemed uncomfortable. "Well, yeah. That's what Mary told her. I should know better than to listen to old woman's gossip."

I laughed, trying to ease his discomfort. "It's actually true. And I would appreciate it if you could put the crib together."

"Great. Would tomorrow be okay?"

I nodded. "Thank you."

"Okay then. I'll see you tomorrow."

I walked him to the door and locked it behind him, then went into the kitchen and began putting everything away. As I placed each item in the cupboard, I smiled, pleased with myself for getting everything back without getting caught by Trevor.

I wondered how he had reacted when Amanda had told him I'd been inside the apartment, and then when he had discovered I'd taken all my kitchen things. I pictured him going into the kitchen to make dinner, opening the cupboard to take out a pan or a casserole dish or a utensil and finding the cupboard bare. I smiled as I imagined him yanking open all the cupboards and drawers and finding them empty. He would kick himself for leaving to meet me. He would probably change the locks now too.

True to his word, Marcus came over first thing the next morning, tools in hand. I led him up to the baby's room, Greta on my heels, and he got right to work on the crib. I wasn't sure if he expected me to keep him company, but I felt I should since he had taken the time to come over and help me out.

Since there was no furniture in the room I sat on the floor and leaned against the wall. Greta pressed herself against me. I had made sure to close the closet door before Marcus came over—I didn't want him, or anyone, to know about the secret room. If they did, it would no longer be a secret, and therefore useless to me.

After working in silence for about ten minutes, Marcus glanced at me and asked when I was due.

"Just before Christmas," I said.

"I can't even tell you're pregnant," he said as he attached two pieces of wood together.

For some reason I felt defensive, like he thought I was making it up. "Well, I am."

He stopped what he was doing and looked at me. "I didn't say you weren't. I just meant . . ." He paused and looked back at what he was doing, then said quietly, "You look really good."

I smiled, feeling foolish for my attitude. "Thanks."

"So, where are you from?"

I almost said Lovelock, but then remembered I'd told his mother I was from Las Vegas. If I'm going to lie, I thought, I'd better keep track of what I tell who. "Vegas."

He glanced at me again. "What brings you here?"

Crap. I'd forgotten to work out a story and would have to make it up on the fly. I knew I needed to keep it simple so I could remember what I'd said. I also thought it would help if I tried to keep it as close to the truth as possible. "Well, my father passed away recently and I felt like I needed a change of scenery, so I packed up and started driving and ended up here." That was actually all true, I thought, proud I'd been able to avoid lying.

"That's cool." He worked for a few more minutes then stopped and looked my way. "Just tell me to mind my own business if you want to, but my mom said Mary told her something about you being a widow."

So much for telling the truth. I nodded and tried to look sad. It was difficult as I had just spoken to my "late husband" the day before. In fact, as I again imagined Trevor's reaction when he'd discovered I'd cleaned out his kitchen I had to bite my lip to keep from smiling.

"I'm sorry," Marcus said as he turned back to his task.

"It's okay," I assured him, a little too brightly.

"It is?" He looked at me, a surprised expression on his face.

Trying to figure out how to cover my lack of grief, I silently berated myself for not thinking before speaking. I would have to improve that habit. Thinking quickly, I said, "What I meant was, even though it was sad when he died, we had been having some trouble for a while and he had recently left me for another woman." That was sort of true.

"Oh. Well excuse me for saying so, but he must have been crazy to cheat on you."

I felt myself blush. "Thanks," I murmured.

A short time later he had the crib put together and he wheeled it against the wall.

"That looks great!" I said. "Thank you so much."

"No problem, Kate."

Just then there was a knock at the door and I felt the blood drain from my face. Greta started barking and took off down the stairs. Marcus was watching me.

"Are you okay?" he asked, clearly concerned.

I hardly heard him as I pictured Trevor waiting on my front porch, fury in his eyes.

The knock sounded again, louder this time.

"Do you want me to get that?" Marcus asked.

Visualizing Trevor's fury turning into outright murderous rage at seeing Marcus answer my door, I quickly shook my head. "No, that's okay." I dashed out of the room, down the stairs, and to the door before Marcus could move. Looking through the peephole, I saw a stranger standing there. Relief cascaded over me in waves and I thought I might pass out from my lightheaded giddiness. I opened the door to see what this stranger wanted.

"Lily Jamison?"

Confused that he knew my real name, I nodded, then glanced behind me to make sure Marcus hadn't overheard. The coast was clear.

"I have a few packages to deliver. Please sign here."

He held out an electronic pad and I signed, remembering the items I'd had shipped from Lovelock. "That was fast." I handed him back the electronic pad.

He grunted in response. "Do you want the boxes inside?"

"Yes, thank you."

As he set the first two boxes on the living room floor, Marcus came down the stairs.

"That's the last one," the man said, setting a box on the floor.

Grateful he hadn't said my name again, I thanked him and watched him leave.

"More garage sales?" Marcus asked, a teasing gleam in his eyes.

I laughed, happy there was no nefarious story behind the appearance of the boxes. "No. I decided to sell my Dad's house and had some things shipped here."

"Oh. Do you need any help moving them someplace else?"

I looked at the stack. I had planned on storing them in the secret room and since I didn't want anyone to know about it, I told him I'd take care of it later.

"You really shouldn't be lifting heavy things. You know, in your condition."

Then it occurred to me that I could have him bring the boxes up to the baby's room. I could push them into the secret room later. "I guess you're right. If it's not too much trouble, could you put them in the baby's room?"

"Sure."

As he reached for the first box I stopped him. "That's actually the TV, so that can stay down here."

I watched as he lifted two boxes at once. His muscles flexed and I couldn't help but feel the pull of his maleness. Trying to push those feelings down, I watched him make several trips up the stairs. Just watching him made me tired and I was glad he had insisted. Finally he came downstairs for the last time. I saw him look at the box that held the TV.

"Would you like me to get that hooked up for you, Kate?"

"Don't you think I've taken up enough of your time?"

He smiled and his startling green eyes drew me in. "Not at all."

"Well, if you don't mind, then I won't object."

After opening the box, he carefully lifted the TV out. "Where do you want it?"

I pointed to where the cable was sticking out of the wall. "The cable's over there."

He walked to where I pointed. "Do you have a table or anything to put it on?"

I shook my head.

"Okay. I'll just put it on the floor for now then."

As he screwed in the cable he glanced my way, then back at what he was doing. "When that guy knocked on the door you looked like you'd seen a ghost." He glanced at me again, apparently waiting for a response.

"Is that a question?" I asked.

"Just an observation."

I nodded, but resisted the urge to tell him everything. It was becoming fairly obvious that the more time I spent with Marcus, the more lies I would have to tell. I decided it would be best to keep our interactions to a minimum.

A short time later he had the TV working. I thanked him and did nothing to encourage him to stay. He left a few minutes later. Within moments of closing the door behind him, intense loneliness washed over me.

CHAPTER FIFTEEN

The next day I decided it was time to start looking for a job. Even though I'd gone online and applied to several retail stores, I hadn't heard back from any of them. Picturing the cute downtown where I'd tried to get a job at the bakery on my first day, I thought I'd check with the places there. I locked Greta in her crate, grabbed my purse and headed out the door.

When I got to the row of stores a few minutes later, I found a parking place and climbed out, glancing up and down the street, wondering where to start. Walking to one end of the street, I went into the first store and approached the counter. The girl at the register smiled at me and asked if she could help me.

"I was wondering if you're hiring," I asked, a friendly smile on my face.

She shook her head. "Not right now. Sorry."

"That's okay. Thanks anyway."

I left that store and went to the next one, repeating the same procedure and getting the same result. After going into half a dozen stores, I was beginning to feel discouraged, but I kept going. When I reached the corner I crossed the street. The first store on this side was a boutique called *Billi's*. Huh, I thought, thinking of my friend Billi.

I pushed the door open and heard a bell ring. As I glanced around I noticed an eclectic collection of vintage clothes and jewelry, as well as funky knick knacks.

"Can I help you?" a voice asked.

I looked at the unfamiliar face and asked the same question I'd asked at all the other stores.

"I don't think we're hiring right now," she said.

I must have looked completely dejected, because she added, "Hang on a second. The owner's in the back. You can ask her."

I nodded, not having much hope. As I waited, I looked through the nearest rack of clothing.

"Kate?"

I spun around, a smile on my face at the sound of the familiar voice. "So this *is* your store!"

Billi smiled back. "Sure is. Maddy here says you're looking for a job." She gestured to the girl I'd spoken to.

"That's right. I haven't had much luck finding one though," I admitted. "You're not hiring by any chance, are you?"

"Actually, I was thinking about bringing another person on part-time. Are you looking for a full-time position?"

Hope surged through me. "No," I quickly answered. "I wouldn't mind full-time, but part-time would be fine too."

"Well then, how would you like to work here?"

I grinned. "I would love it."

"Great! Can you start tomorrow?"

"Yeah. What time would you like me to be here?"

"I need someone for the early shift, so say, eight o'clock in the morning?"

"That sounds perfect."

"All right then. Bring your social security card and driver's license and we'll get everything started in the morning."

"Sounds good. I'll see you then."

I left the store feeling fantastic. I had a job! And Billi would be my boss. We hadn't spent very much time talking in the dog obedience class or the self-defense class, but she'd been friendly to me. I looked forward to getting to know her better.

Then I thought about showing her my social security card and driver's license and a wave of worry washed over me. I pushed it aside, knowing there was no other option.

When I got home I tried to use my last full day off to get everything organized. After playing with Greta in the backyard for a while, I went into the baby's room, slid open the closet, and opened the entrance to the secret room. All of the boxes that Marcus had brought up to the room were stacked neatly in a corner of the baby's room. One by one I moved them into the secret room for storage, then I secured the door.

As I was about to slide the closet door closed, I noticed the light that seeped around the edges of the small door and realized if Trevor was looking for me, that light could give away my position. Going to the linen closet, I dug around and found a blanket, then brought it into the secret room. Holding up the blanket, I considered how to hang it over the door, then noticed several nails sticking out of the wall above the door.

After folding the blanket into fourths, I pressed the fabric against the nails until holes formed and the blanket hung securely over the door. Then I got on my hands and knees and, pushing the blanket aside, crawled out of the secret room. I closed the small door behind me and stood back, examining the door for any sign of light. It was completely dark around the door now.

Satisfied that I had disguised the fact that a large room lay hidden behind the door, I pushed the boxes against the door and slid the closet door closed. Then I turned and faced the baby's room.

As I looked around, I made a mental list of the items I would need for when the baby came: a dresser and changing table, a rocking chair, a mattress for the crib, as well as linens and a few baby outfits. The thought of buying all of those things didn't stress me out quite as much, now that I knew I would have some income.

Now that my home felt organized, I wanted to relax. I pulled out my laptop and went online and immediately pulled up my email account. As I saw the inevitable email from Trevor, my heart pounded. I knew I had been putting off checking for an email from him since I'd gotten back from Reno. The thought of his reaction to my tricking him scared me.

With trepidation, I clicked on the email.

Dear Lily,

I know you probably expect me to be mad about what you did, but honestly I'm not.

I stopped, shocked by what Trevor had said. I reread it to make sure I hadn't misunderstood, then continued on.

I would have done the same thing if I were you. I know that stuff was yours and I don't begrudge you taking it. I can't tell you how disappointed I was to get to Circus Circus and find out you weren't there. I know I haven't done a lot to deserve your trust, but I really thought you wanted to see me. I know you don't believe me, but I still love you so much! I want us to be a family again. Please, Lily. Please tell me where you are. I want to be with you so bad that it hurts.

All my love,

Trevor

I stared at his message, overwhelmed with confusion. He had reacted completely opposite of what I had been prepared for. I had expected him to be furious with me and to say how much he hated me and wanted to hurt me. I had been prepared for that. But his expression of love and understanding had taken me completely by surprise and I didn't know how to react.

As I thought about his words, then remembered Amanda telling me that Trevor didn't love me anymore, I wondered what to believe. It hadn't looked like Amanda was living there, so maybe she was just saying what she thought and not what Trevor had said. Then I remembered Trevor kissing her before he came to meet me. That image didn't seem to match up to the love he had professed in his email.

What was I supposed to believe? The words he told me or the actions I saw? In either case, I felt he had betrayed me by being with Amanda. It's true that I had left him and he could do what he wanted, but if he loved me so much, why was he with her?

When I visualized them embracing and Trevor kissing her and then her acting like I was the intruder in my apartment, fury spread throughout my body. Taking several deep breaths, I forced myself to calm down, worried I could hurt the baby by letting my emotions get so out of control.

Without thinking, I hit the Reply button and composed an email to Trevor.

Trevor,

If you love me so much, why are you with Amanda now? And why did you tell her to not let me leave?

Lily

I hit Send before I had a chance to change my mind. I had to know why he was with Amanda.

Shutting down my computer, I turned on the TV and flipped through the channels before finding a show that looked interesting. I watched TV for a while, then fixed myself something to eat. When it was time for bed I took my eReader, the one Trevor had gotten me for Christmas, and brought it to bed. As I selected a book, I remembered the day he'd given it to me. It was the same day I had told him I would marry him. We had been so happy. It was hard to believe how much had changed in such a short period of time.

I read for a while, then turned off the light, excited to start my new job the next morning.

Chapter Sixteen

I arrived at *Billi's* right at eight o'clock. She met me at the door and invited me in.

"We probably have a little time before any customers come in. Let's go in back and get the paperwork filled out."

I followed her through the small store and into the office tucked in the back. She sat at the desk and invited me to sit in the extra chair.

"Do you have your driver's license and social security card?"

"Yes." I pulled them out of my wallet and handed them to her, nervous about what she would say. I watched as she looked them over, then she looked at me.

"I don't understand. This says your name is Lily."

"Well, that's my legal name," I said. "Kate is my nickname."

She seemed to accept that. "Okay."

She had me fill out some other paperwork and after I'd signed where required, she smiled at me. "That's it. Let me show you around."

After going over where things were and what some of the procedures were, she told me to let her know if I needed any help and then went back into her office. I wandered around, making myself familiar with the inventory. As I was examining some decorative items on one of the shelves, I heard the bell tinkle as a customer entered the store.

"How may I help you?" I asked the woman.

She told me what she was looking for and I spent the next fifteen minutes helping her. More customers came in and I stayed busy until it was time for me to leave at one o'clock. I said good-bye to Billi and she told me my assigned days to work. As I drove home, I smiled, satisfied with my morning. I had enjoyed working at *Billi's* boutique and looked forward to working there the next day.

The first thing I did when I got home was to let Greta out of her crate. She was ecstatic to see me. We went out back and I threw the ball with her and worked with her on some of the training techniques we'd learned. She'd been doing really well and I thought she might be ready to be left out of her crate when I was at work. I would be gone less than six hours. Even so, I knew I would feel better if she had a way to get in and out of the house on her own.

I grabbed my cell phone and dialed Mary's number. After the pleasantries, I asked how she would feel if I put a dog door in the kitchen door that went out to the backyard. To my pleasure, she agreed, saying I could always replace the door itself if needed. I thought that was fair. We hung up and I smiled in Greta's direction.

"Greta, you're going to get your very own door. How does that sound?"

Greta stood next to me, her tail wagging, waiting for me to throw the ball again.

As a test, I left Greta out back while I went to the pet store to buy a dog door. I wanted to see how she would do outside on her own. I'd never left her alone out back before, but if she was going to have the ability to go in and out on her own, she would be able to go out back and I needed to see what she would do.

Less than an hour later I was back. Hurrying inside, I went straight to the backyard and flung open the back door, expecting to be jumped on by a happy dog. Instead, I was startled to see Marcus sitting on my back porch, playing with Greta.

"What are you doing here?" I blurted.

"Hi, Kate."

I stepped onto the porch and stood with my hands on my hips.

The way he had just shown up like that was reminiscent of Trevor and it made me very nervous. "Why are you in my backyard?"

"I'm really sorry," he said, apparently sensing my anger.

His sincere expression of remorse calmed me and I sat on the porch steps nearby. "It just freaked me out to see you in my backyard."

"I only came over because Greta was barking so much. I'd never heard her do that before and I was worried something was wrong. I came over to check on you and when I found her in the backyard by herself, I wondered what had happened."

Touched by his genuine concern, I smiled. Then I laughed and shook a finger at Greta. "You're a naughty girl. You shouldn't be barking like that." She rushed over to me and pushed her nose into my hand, encouraging me to pet her, which I did. Then I looked at Marcus. "I left her outside on purpose to see what she would do. I started a new job today and I'm going to put in a dog door so she'll be able to come in and out on her own and I wanted to see how she would react to being outside by herself."

He nodded. "Oh, okay. Hey, congrats on the job, by the way. Where is it?"

"At *Billi's* boutique, downtown. Do you know where it is?"

"Yeah." He paused. "Where are you putting the dog door?"

"In the back door there." I pointed to the door that led into the kitchen.

"Have you done that kind of thing before?"

"Well no. But maybe you can teach me?"

He grinned. "Let me just get my tools."

I watched him push himself off of the porch and head toward the back gate. While I waited for him to return, I tossed the ball for Greta a few times. When the gate opened, I saw Marcus come through, a box of tools in one hand.

First he traced the outline of the dog door on the kitchen door, marking where we would need to cut, then he held up the jigsaw and showed me how it worked. He started cutting, then stopped.

"You try it." He handed me the jigsaw.

Hesitating, I just looked at it. "But what if I mess up?"

"Here, I'll help you. Hold the jigsaw like this."

He demonstrated and when he handed the jigsaw to me, I mimicked his example.

"Now put the blade through the cut I started."

I pushed the blade into the narrow area where he had begun cutting.

"Now squeeze the trigger that's by your finger."

Nervous I would either mess up what he'd done so far, or cut myself, I gently squeezed the trigger. The jigsaw's movement startled me and I almost dropped it. I let go of the trigger and looked at Marcus to see his reaction. I expected to see him scowling at me—after all, this was his tool and I could easily damage it. But when my eyes met his, he looked like he was trying to hold back a laugh. "What's so funny?" I asked, now feeling dumb.

"It's okay," he assured me. "Sometimes it takes practice."

Feeling a little better, I tried it again, but again it seemed to buck in my hands. "I don't think I can do this." I tried to hand the jigsaw back to him, but he shook his head.

"I can help you, if it's okay," he said.

I didn't know exactly what he meant, so I agreed. Then he knelt behind me, put his arms on either side of me, and then put his hands over mine. His muscular arms pressed against me and the scent of his cologne filled my senses. Heat pulsed through me and I tensed, not knowing what to do.

He didn't seem to notice and with his mouth right by my ear he said, "Okay, now squeeze the trigger."

My heart pounding, and not from using the jigsaw, I did as he asked and he guided my hands so that the jigsaw cut where it was supposed to. The sensation of the jigsaw vibrating in our hands, and

Marcus pressed against me, made my heart race. We finished cutting out the space where the dog door would go and he let go of my hands, then backed away. I handed him the jigsaw and he smiled at me. I noticed his gorgeous green eyes seemed to sparkle and I wondered what he had felt when he'd been so close to me.

"You did it, Kate." He had a big smile on his face.

Still unnerved by having him so close to me, I tentatively smiled back. "Only because you helped me."

"I enjoyed helping you," he said, a twinkle in his eyes.

I felt myself blush, and then guilt suffused me. After all, I was a married woman. I felt like I was cheating on Trevor. But I couldn't blame Marcus—he believed I was single. And if Trevor was cheating on me with Amanda, and if I had no intention of getting back together with Trevor, was it really cheating? I pushed my concerns aside. It really didn't matter anyway. All I was interested in was taking care of myself and my baby. Getting involved with anyone was out of the question. Even so, I could enjoy Marcus' friendship. And I could do it without fear of reprisals from Trevor.

"So what's next?" I asked, trying to make it clear this was all business for me, although inside I was completely out of sorts.

"Now we attach the door. Do you want to try it?" He held the dog door in one hand and his drill in the other.

I shook my head. "No, that's okay."

"All right." Marcus put the door in the opening, then secured it in place. He turned to me. "That's it. Greta can use it now."

"Hear that, Greta?" I scratched her head, finally feeling in control of my emotions. "You have your own door now. Let's see if you can use it." I went into the house and closed the door, leaving her on the outside. Then I lifted the dog door from my side and encouraged her to come through. Poking her nose through, she hesitated, then she stepped through and I let the flap fall down.

Marcus did the same thing from his side and she went back

outside. "I think she's got it," he said.

I went back onto the porch and praised Greta. Then I smiled at Marcus. "Thanks for all your help. Again." I couldn't help but feel guilty for all the help he'd given me and I wondered what I could to do to show my appreciation. "What can I do to pay you back for all you've done?"

He grinned, like he'd already thought of this. "You can let me take you out to dinner."

Though caught off guard by his request, I forced the smile to stay on my face, but I could feel it faltering. He must have seen it too.

Looking disappointed, he said, "That's okay. You don't have to."

Now I felt even worse. He'd done so much to help me, how could I turn down his invitation? Saying no would make me look ungrateful and that's not how I was feeling at all. If he hadn't helped me bring the crib in the house and put it together and carry all those heavy boxes upstairs, and now put in the dog door for Greta, what would I have done? Telling him no would be selfish. "Of course, Marcus. I'd love to go to dinner with you."

The sparkle returned to his green eyes as a smile lit his face. "Great! What night works best for you?"

"Well, tonight I have Greta's obedience school and tomorrow I have my self-defense class."

"Self-defense? I didn't know you were taking a class. What made you want to do that?"

"Well, you know," I stammered. "It's just that I live here by myself."

He nodded, accepting my answer. "You know, Kate, I learned some hand-to-hand combat techniques in the marines. I can always teach you some of those."

"Oh. I'd like that." I figured it wouldn't hurt to learn a few more moves, in addition to the ones Steve was teaching me in class. Especially after I'd actually put those moves to use to get away from

Amanda. The thought of having to get away from Trevor, who was bigger and stronger than me, made me realize that I could use all the training I could get.

"But anyway. About dinner?"

"Yes," I said. "Thursday or Friday would work."

"Let's plan on Thursday. I'll come by about six, if that's okay."

"Sounds great," I said, smiling. I found I was looking forward to getting to know Marcus better. But just as a friend, of course.

CHAPTER SEVENTEEN

That night at dog obedience school I chatted with Billi before we started. Though I'd spent the morning working at her store, she'd either been in the back office or helping customers, so we hadn't talked much. And though she'd been kind to me, I hadn't told her anything about my past. As far as I knew, she didn't even know I was pregnant. I knew it would be obvious soon enough, so I really needed to tell her, but the right moment hadn't presented itself yet.

Following the instructions of the teacher, I took Greta through her paces and she did well. I knew she would need another course when she got older, but she was getting the basics down. By the time class was over I was exhausted. It had been my busiest day yet. I'd started my new job, then worked with Marcus to put in the dog door, and then come to class.

As I said good-bye to Billi and her dog Chloe, and walked Greta to my car, I thought about Marcus and the way he'd made me feel when he'd helped me use the jigsaw. Heat raced through me as I recalled the sensation of having him so close. But how could I feel that way when it had only been a month since I'd left Trevor? Confused by my feelings, I shook my head as I helped Greta into my car and drove home.

I hadn't had a chance to check my email before going to class, but after having a snack I booted up my laptop and went online and immediately opened my email. There was an email from Trevor. I opened it to see if he'd answered my questions about Amanda.

Lily,

I think you misunderstood what you saw. I'm not "with" Amanda. She just happened to stop by when you were there. She's just a friend. It's you I love! And honestly, I don't know what you mean when you said Amanda said I told her not to let you leave. I didn't tell her anything like that. The only thing I can figure is that I said I hoped you wouldn't leave before I got back. She must have misunderstood me.

Please Lily! Please know how much I love you and miss you. I want to be with you so much. You and our baby. Please reconsider what you're doing. Please, just tell me where you are and I can come and get you and bring you home to be with me.

Love always, your husband,

Trevor

Now I was more confused than ever. Did he really love me? Was he telling the truth about Amanda or did he just not know that I'd seen him kissing her? Did he really not tell Amanda to keep me there until he got back? Or was he just trying to trick me? And if he was trying to trick me, why would he? What did he want from me? Did he want revenge because I'd taken my money back? Did he really want to be part of our baby's life? I had no idea what his real agenda was. Half of me wanted to believe him, because then maybe there was a chance for us. But the other half wanted to forget I'd ever known him so I could move on with my life and not have all of the uncertainty that he was throwing at me.

I felt like I was making a life for myself here and even though I felt lonely a lot of the time, at least I felt relatively safe. And most importantly I had my freedom. Trevor was out of his mind if he thought I would tell him where I was.

Exhausted, and not wanting to deal with Trevor just then, I shut down my laptop and went to bed.

As I lay in bed that night I realized I was two different people. One of my personas was Lily, Trevor's pregnant and estranged wife. A woman in hiding from her husband. A woman emailing her husband and fighting to figure out what he really wanted from her. A woman desperate to keep her baby safe and to keep her husband from finding her.

Then there was Kate. As Kate, I played the grieving, pregnant widow. A woman who valiantly lived on her own. A woman who worked part-time, owned a dog, took self-defense classes, and had a devastatingly handsome neighbor who liked to come over and help the poor, helpless young widow.

In the privacy of my room I allowed the tears to come. Who did I want to be? Who was I hurting by playacting? What would happen when my baby was born? I couldn't go on like this forever. Eventually the truth was bound to come out. But right now I really loved being Kate. I didn't want to be Lily anymore. I wanted Lily to disappear. I wanted to pretend like Trevor had never happened.

Right then I vowed to ignore Trevor's emails. If I wanted to be Kate, then Trevor could not exist in my life. Feeling marginally better once I'd decided on a solution, I was able to drift off to sleep.

The next morning at work I enjoyed helping the customers. Billi worked in her office unless it got busy, then she came out and helped customers. I hoped to have the chance to talk to her sometime soon.

That night was my self-defense class, and after my run-in with Amanda I paid extra close attention to the instructions. I felt more confident as I practiced, although I didn't exactly feel ready to face off with Trevor if it came to that. Even though I had decided to ignore his emails, I wasn't so blind as to think I shouldn't be prepared for whatever may happen in the future.

I thought I might have a chance to talk to Billi, but she left early. The next day at work I told her I needed to talk to her for a few minutes when she had some time. She suggested we chat when my shift was over and Maddy came in.

As the end of my shift approached I became more nervous about the conversation I was going to have with Billi. Would she be angry with me for not telling her about my pregnancy before she hired me? In the few conversations we'd had I had discovered she was single and childless. Did that mean she didn't think children were a good idea?

"Kate, I'm available now," Billi said, motioning for me to come into her office.

I took a deep breath and followed her in. She sat in her desk chair and I sat in the extra chair.

"How do you like working here?" she asked.

I smiled. "I really like it."

"Good. The customers seem to like you, and you're doing a great job."

I relaxed under her praise. "Thank you."

"Now, what was it you wanted to talk about?"

Her face was open and friendly and I hoped my fears had been misplaced. "There was something I needed to tell you." I paused, gathering my courage. "I'm pregnant." I watched several different emotions play across her face. "I'm sorry I didn't tell you before you hired me," I rushed to say. "I was just so excited for the chance to work here that I didn't even think about it."

"When are you due?"

"Not until Christmas."

"So you're planning on working up until then?"

"Yeah. I'm, uh, I'm planning on going to school in the fall, but I was going to schedule afternoon classes so it wouldn't interfere with working here."

"I see."

Afraid now that she would fire me, I bit my lip.

"Well, my concern is that I can count on you to be here when you're scheduled."

"That won't be a problem," I hurried to assure her.

"But it might be a problem if you can't work during the Christmas rush."

"I should be available at least through the middle of December though."

"I guess we'll just see how it goes. I usually have to hire extra staff for Christmas, so I'll just keep your issues in mind."

"I appreciate you hiring me, Billi."

She smiled. "I don't regret it. Just keep up the good work and I'm sure everything will work out."

I thanked her and said good-bye, then drove home, relieved our meeting had gone well and that I still had a job.

When I got home I played with Greta. So far she had been doing fine on her own when I was at work, which made me happy. As I threw the ball for her my eyes strayed in the direction of Marcus' house. No one was outside at his house. I turned my attention back to Greta and smiled. That night Marcus would be taking me to dinner.

CHAPTER EIGHTEEN

At six o'clock I heard a knock at the door. Excited to be going to dinner with Marcus, I hurried to answer. He wore a button down shirt that emphasized his amazing green eyes.

"You look very nice, Kate," he said, a smile on his face.

"Thanks." I followed him out to his car, an older model black jeep. He opened the door for me and I climbed in. When he slid behind the wheel I said, "It doesn't seem quite right that you're taking *me* to dinner, when I'm the one who is supposed to be thanking you."

He grinned at me. "Well, I'd like to think I'm a gentleman, and a gentleman takes a lady to dinner, not the other way around."

I returned his smile. "Okay. I guess I can live with that."

"Good." He turned the key in the ignition as I put on my seatbelt, then he backed down the gravel drive and pulled onto the road that ran in front of our houses. A short time later we pulled into a parking space at the restaurant.

When he turned the jeep off, I reached for the door handle.

"Hang on, Kate."

I watched as he jumped out of the jeep and hurried around to my side of the vehicle, opening the door for me. Then he held out his hand to help me from the car.

I couldn't help but smirk a little. "Wow. You really are a gentleman, aren't you?"

A slow smile spread across his face. "I try to be."

Then he held out his arm for me to take, which I did, and we went into the restaurant. We didn't have to wait long to be seated. The server approached and asked if she could start us off with a drink or an appetizer. I noticed that Marcus just asked for water and I wondered if he drank much. I decided I would try to find out.

After we gave our orders and the server left, Marcus focused on me. "Tell me about yourself, Kate."

"I think you already know the basics."

He smiled. "I know you're from Vegas and that you moved here on a whim. I know you're going to have a baby in December and that your husband passed away. I know you have a dog named Greta and that you just started working at *Billi's* and that you're taking a self-defense class." He paused, a twinkle in his eyes. "And I know you need more practice with the jigsaw before you take on any large projects."

Heat raced up my face as I remembered the feeling of his arms around me when he helped me with Greta's dog door.

As he saw my discomfort, his smile grew. "It's okay. I didn't mind helping."

It felt like my cheeks reddened even more, if that was possible. I looked down at the napkin in my lap as I tried to regain my composure.

He laughed, clearly amused. "You're cute when you blush, Kate."

I lifted my gaze to meet his and tried to hold back a smile. "I'm glad you find it so amusing."

"I'm sorry. I just call it like I see it." His smile didn't waver.

"It sounds like you know everything there is to know about me, so tell me more about you," I said, trying to turn the focus away from myself.

The server set our water on the table and we watched her walk away.

"So?" I prompted.

"Okay. I told you before that I recently came home from Afghanistan."

I nodded.

"I've been in the marines since I was eighteen, but now I'm ready to do some other things."

"How long were you in the military?"

"Six years."

He's twenty-four, I thought. Three years older than me. "What made you decide to leave?"

"I'd done several tours and felt for me, it was time to move on to other things."

"So what are your plans now?"

"College. I earned some college funds through my military service and now I want to put it to good use."

I smiled. "That's great! Do you know what you want to major in?"

"Electrical engineering."

Just then the server brought our food, and our conversation slowed down while we ate.

Marcus set his fork down. "So, Kate. What's in the future for you?"

I swallowed what I'd been chewing and set my fork down as well. "I'm planning on taking some college courses this fall. I'd really like to get my Bachelor's degree, but with the baby coming, I'm not sure when I'll be able to get that done."

"Wanting to get it done is the first step though."

I nodded, glad his attitude toward education was similar to mine.

"Do you know what you want to major in?" he asked, resuming his eating.

"I enjoy working with computers, so I was thinking something in IT."

His eyebrows went up, like he was impressed, and I felt my confidence grow. "That's awesome, Kate."

"So Marcus, tell me, what do you do all day? Besides help me out, I mean."

"I'd like to spend all day helping you out," he said, grinning. "But actually I've been job hunting. And I think one of the jobs I applied for might just work out. I'll actually find out tomorrow."

"That's great. What kind of a job is it?"

"It's kind of like an internship, but it would be a permanent position at an engineering firm."

Now I was the one who was impressed. "That sounds very promising."

"Yeah. I had some training in the marines and I really liked it."

"I hope it works out for you."

"Thanks."

He lifted his water glass to his lips and took a sip. I decided if I wanted to know how he felt about drinking, I would just have to come out and ask. "So, Marcus."

He set his drink down. "Yes?"

"I noticed that you just got water. Don't you like to drink?"

He glanced down, then to the side, then back at me. I wondered why he seemed so uncomfortable and felt suddenly worried that he would be another Trevor.

"You know, I'm actually not a big fan of drinking," he finally said.

That was not what I had been expecting at all and I was elated. "Really?"

He looked hesitant. "Does that bother you?"

I smiled and he seemed to relax. "Not at all. I'm curious why though."

"I don't know. Getting drunk and losing control never really appealed to me."

I thought of all of the things I'd found out about him: education was important to him, he had good career prospects, he didn't like to drink, and he was gorgeous. Of course I had already known about that last one. But as I thought about how much he filled my list of qualities I wanted in a man, I felt my heart sing.

Then my other self, Lily, forced her way into my head. *You're married, remember?*

But I didn't want to be Lily. I wanted to be Kate. And never as much as right now. Pushing those thoughts aside, I focused on Marcus, who was watching me.

"So, Kate. How do you feel about drinking?"

Pulling myself back to the moment, I almost laughed. It seemed like he was the one now who was worried that I might not measure up. "Well, the reason I asked you is because I have strong feelings on drinking. When I was little my mother was killed by a drunk driver, so I kind of frown on drinking."

"Oh. I'm sorry to hear about your mother. I had no idea."

"That's okay. I don't really remember much about her."

"What about your dad? What does he do?"

The elation I had been feeling moments before was swiftly replaced by sadness and I knew it showed on my face. I couldn't help it. His question reminded me that whether I was Lily or Kate, I still had no family left in the world.

"Are you okay?" he asked, obviously noticing my distress.

I nodded, trying to control my emotions. I cleared my throat, giving myself a moment to collect myself. "He passed away last year."

Marcus' hand reached across the table and held mine. A jolt of electricity shot up my arm at his touch. I wondered if he felt it too or if it was just one-sided.

"Wow. You've really had a lot of bad luck lately." Then a look of optimism appeared on his face. "But I have a good feeling, Kate. Good things are in store for you."

Somehow that made me feel better and I smiled. "Thanks."

He pulled his hand back to his side of the table and I missed the strength and warmth it had offered. The server appeared and asked if we wanted dessert. When we had both said no, she set the check down. Marcus grabbed it before I had a chance to even consider paying.

As we drove back to our neighborhood we chatted about nothing in particular. A short time later we pulled in front of my house.

Marcus walked me to the door. "I really enjoyed having dinner with you, Kate."

I gazed into his eyes and felt inexorably drawn to him. "Me, too. Thanks for taking me. And thanks again for all the help you've given me."

He grinned. "No problem."

"Let me know what happens with that job you were telling me about."

"I will."

I desperately wanted him to kiss me, but I also knew I'd feel terribly guilty if he did. Even though Trevor might choose to cheat on me with Amanda, I knew I couldn't do the same. As long as I was married, I knew I needed to keep Marcus at arm's length. I turned toward the door and put my key in the lock. I started to open the door, then turned back toward Marcus. "Thanks again for everything."

"Take care, Kate."

I couldn't tell if he'd wanted to kiss me or not, but he seemed to understand that I wasn't making myself available. I watched him walk to his jeep and drive away.

I went inside and found Greta there to meet me. "I can always depend on you," I said, scratching her head.

Even though I had decided to pretend Trevor didn't exist, I realized that if I truly wanted to get on with my life, I would need to make a clean break from him. I booted up my laptop and opened my email account. I hit Reply on his last message, the one where he claimed he wasn't "with" Amanda.

Trevor,

You need to understand that we will never get back together. You literally made me a prisoner in my home. You stole my inheritance money. You lied to me and you lied to your parents about me. And you hurt me. You pushed me down. You didn't know it at the time, but I was pregnant. You could have hurt your own child. I can't be with you anymore.

Trevor, I want a divorce. Please understand that this will be in the best interest of both of us.

Lily

I pressed Send before I had a chance to dwell on the message I was sending.

Chapter Nineteen

As soon as I got home from work the next afternoon I checked my email account. Trevor had responded. With trepidation I opened the message.

Lily,

I'm sorry you feel that way because that's not how I feel. I see a future for us. But I'll tell you what, if you tell me where you are and we can meet face to face, I'll consider it.

I still love you,

Trevor

I hadn't really expected he would agree with me, but I'd hoped he might. There was no way I would tell him where I was and I was extremely hesitant to meet with him face to face. I opened another tab in my browser and Googled divorce in California. After doing a little research I discovered that I would have to be a resident of California for at least six months before I could file for divorce. Even though it would have been good to know that before I told Trevor I wanted a divorce, at least I had made my wishes known. Maybe in another five months, when my six month residency was met, he would be willing to agree.

Then I researched getting a divorce in Nevada. It would be much easier there. Only one of us had to be a resident of Nevada. However, either I would have to live there for six weeks to qualify, or Trevor would have to be the one to file. Right now I didn't have much hope of that happening. And it looked like the fact that I was pregnant with his child would complicate things.

Maybe I should hire an attorney, I thought. But I didn't want to go that route just yet.

I shut down my computer, frustrated that my life was at this point. A year ago I could never have imagined myself in this situation. I was starting to feel sorry for myself.

"Greta, let's go play." I jumped up from the couch and walked to the back door. Greta followed eagerly behind. We went outside and played until I had pushed my troubles with Trevor to the back of my mind.

When I came back inside I started dinner. As I was waiting for a chicken breast to bake, I heard a knock at the door. Greta immediately raced to the door, barking. Even though she was still a puppy, she had a strong bark. The sound of it made me feel safer. I walked to the door, not feeling quite as jumpy as I had in the past. After peeking through the peephole I opened the door to see Marcus standing on my porch, a big grin on his face.

His smile was contagious and I smiled back. "What?" I asked.

"I got the job."

"That's great! Congratulations! Do you want to come in?" He followed me into the living room and we sat on the couch. "So when do you start?"

"Monday. And it's a really great job."

I could see how excited he was and I wanted to give him a hug in congratulations, but I hesitated, not wanting him to get the wrong idea.

"I knew you would get it," I said with enthusiasm. "As soon as you told me about it, I just had a feeling."

"Me, too. But I didn't want to get my hopes up." He paused. "The reason I came over, besides to tell you about the job, was to see if you'd come have dinner with my family on Sunday night. Kind of a celebration about the job."

"Sure," I said, without hesitation. His mother, Trish, had been kind to me and I thought it would be nice to spend an evening with his family. And I wanted to support him in his good news. After all, that's what friends did.

"Great! We eat a little early on Sunday. About five."

I nodded. "I'll be there." I paused. "Does your mom want me to bring anything?"

"No, I don't think so."

"Okay."

Just then the timer went off, indicating my chicken was done. The smell coming from the kitchen left no doubt that I had been preparing dinner.

"Well, I'll let you get to your dinner, Kate."

I was tempted to invite him to eat with me, but I had only made enough food for me. Anyway, I told myself, you need to keep things platonic. You're already eating dinner with Marcus and his family on Sunday. And you just had dinner with him last night. No need to overdo it.

Marcus stood and walked toward the door and I followed. "Congratulations again. I know you'll do great."

"Thanks, Kate," he said, a broad smile on his face.

After he left I ate my meal, then watched television for a while. Finally, I booted up my laptop and composed a response to Trevor's email.

Trevor,

I feel like you're trying to blackmail me into meeting with you. That's not going to happen. Please don't contact me again unless you're ready to move forward with the divorce.

Lily

I hit Send and hoped for the best.

CHAPTER TWENTY

Billi had given me the weekend off, which was nice. Taking advantage of the free time, I drove around and checked out garage sales —I still needed a dresser and changing table for the baby. Even though I started early, it seemed most of the good stuff was gone by the time I showed up, although I found a nice table lamp, which I would put on top of the baby's dresser, once I found one.

Once home, I took Greta for a walk around the neighborhood and practiced some of the things we'd learned in her obedience school. She only had one lesson left before this phase of her training was done. She hadn't had any more accidents, which I was grateful for, but she was still working on learning how to stay and how to keep from jumping on my visitors. But she kept me company and I was glad to have her.

Before I knew it, it was time to have dinner with Marcus and his parents. Even though Marcus said I didn't need to bring anything, I made a plate of brownies. This would be my first time meeting Marcus' dad and I wanted to make a good impression on him and Trish. Though Marcus and I were just friends, I wanted my neighbors to think well of me.

I walked over to their house, balancing the plate in my hands, and rang the doorbell. After only a moment I heard footsteps approach and I started to feel nervous. Marcus opened the door, a big smile on his face.

"Hey, Kate. Come in."

He opened the door wider and I walked in. Glancing around, I noticed that it was nicely decorated, in a subdued way.

"Where would you like these?" I held out the brownies.

"You didn't need to bring anything."

"I know, but I wanted to."

He took them from me.

"Hi, Kate," Trish said, coming to greet me.

A tall man that looked like an older version of Marcus stood behind her.

"Kate, this is my husband, Jeff," Trish said.

"Hi," I said.

"Welcome." He smiled warmly, then invited me to come out to the backyard, where they were grilling salmon. We all chatted as we waited for the food to cook, then sat at the table to eat.

Marcus' family was really nice and I enjoyed their company. Their kindness reminded me of Trevor's parents and I felt guilt wash over me at the thought that his parents probably didn't know anything about what was going on between Trevor and me. I seriously doubted he would have told them. I hoped I would be able to include them in my baby's life though.

"I understand you're from Vegas," Jeff was saying to me.

I nodded, not quite able to verbalize the lie, especially when they were being so friendly to me.

"How do you like it here so far?"

I smiled, glad I could be completely honest in my answer. "I love it. Everyone I've met has been so friendly and I'm really enjoying my little place." I glanced at Marcus. "And your son has been kind enough to help me with a few projects. I've really appreciated all he's done."

I noticed Marcus' parents glance at him with a knowing smile. I wondered what secret they were keeping, but knew I had enough secrets of my own to keep me busy.

Jeff turned back to me. "Marcus has always been handy to have around."

After dessert we played board games. I hadn't done that since before Dad developed his dementia. Playing games with Marcus' family brought back all kinds of good memories. Finally it was time to go home. I thanked Jeff and Trish for having me over.

When it became clear that I was leaving, Marcus offered to walk me home. Even though I felt perfectly safe walking home alone, I didn't want to hurt his feelings by saying no. Besides, if I was honest with myself, I had to admit that I enjoyed being with him. Maybe a bit too much.

"Your family's really nice," I said as we walked side by side down the street that ran in front of our houses.

"Yeah, most of the time."

I looked at him, surprised by his response. "What do you mean?"

"You know how it is with parents. We don't always agree on everything."

I didn't know what he meant. I'd been without parents for a year and before that, while Dad suffered through his dementia, he hadn't been himself and I'd actually been the adult in our relationship during that time. And before he'd become sick, he'd been too busy putting food on the table to watch my every move and argue with me. Of course I'd been too busy going to high school and running our household to have a chance to get into trouble.

"I guess," I finally said.

Marcus glanced at me and I could tell he'd just realized the faux pas he'd committed, talking about parents like that when I didn't have any.

"I'm so sorry, Kate. That was really insensitive of me."

"It's okay," I quickly assured him. "You don't need to walk on eggshells around me. Life is what it is. There's no need to not talk about your parents just because mine happen to no longer be around."

We reached the gravel drive that led to my house. Marcus stopped and turned toward me. "Kate, there's something really special about you."

I smiled, suffused with warmth at his words. "Thanks."

Then he took my hand and continued walking. Powerful waves of attraction rolled up my arm and spread throughout my body. When we reached my porch, he turned toward me, one of my hands still in his. Then he reached out and took my other hand as well. As I gazed into his amazing green eyes, I felt myself nearly sway in his direction. He held my gaze with his and I wondered what he was thinking. Was he going to kiss me? What was stopping him? What would I do if he did kiss me? Or if he didn't? The tension in waiting to see what he would do was agonizing.

Finally he smiled and blinked, then said, "Thanks for having dinner with my family."

He relaxed his grip on my hands, letting them slide out of his. Evidently there would be no kiss tonight. The Lily in me felt relief, but the Kate in me was completely disappointed.

With my hands freed, I reached into my pocket and extracted the key. I could hear Greta moving around on the other side of the door. I unlocked the door and opened it, letting Greta bound out. She greeted me by trying to jump on me. I pushed her down with my knee against her chest and said "Down" in a commanding voice, just as I'd been shown. Then she turned to Marcus and tried the same thing. "You need to push your knee against her chest to show her that she shouldn't do that."

He looked at me with a question in his eyes. "I don't want to hurt her though."

"Just do it gently. She'll get the message eventually."

As she continued trying to jump on him, he tried to do as I'd instructed, but he was too tall and his knee was too high to touch her chest. We both laughed at his attempt.

"Never mind," I laughed.

"Maybe when she's bigger," he said, smiling.

"Well hopefully by then she'll know better than to jump on people."

"Yeah, I guess it would be a lot worse if she was doing that when she's bigger."

We stood there for a moment, watching Greta. Finally I said, "Thanks for dinner. I had fun."

He smiled. "Take care, Kate."

I watched as he turned and started walking back down the gravel drive. "Good luck at work tomorrow," I called out.

He stopped and looked at me. "Thanks." Then he continued on.

CHAPTER TWENTY-ONE

The next afternoon after I'd been home from work for a while, Trish stopped by.

"You forgot this," she said, holding the plate I'd used for the brownies.

"Oh, thank you." I took the plate from her, then asked if she wanted to come in.

"Yes," she said. "There's actually something I want to talk to you about."

"Okay." I led her to the couch, then took the plate into the kitchen and set it on the counter before coming back into the living room. Greta was being her usual friendly self. I pulled her away from Trish and got her to settle down on her pet bed, then I sat on the other end of the couch.

"She's gotten bigger since I saw her last," Trish said.

"Yeah. I guess she has. It's harder for me to notice since I see her all the time."

Trish nodded. "Kate, the reason I wanted to talk to you, is to, well, to ask you kind of a favor."

"Okay."

"I know it's really not my place to get involved in my son's relationships."

"There is no relationship between Marcus and me," I interrupted. "We're just friends."

"I see."

The way she said it made me wonder exactly what she saw. Had Marcus told her something else? Was I dealing with another Trevor? Someone who would lie to his parents about me? I didn't want to depend on someone else to clear up misconceptions about me, like I had with Trevor and his mother, so I decided to make sure Trish and I were on the same page. "I don't know what Marcus has told you about our friendship, but that's all it is. We're just friends. Nothing more."

Trish seemed taken aback by my statement. "Marcus hasn't actually told me anything."

I was glad to hear that, but it made me wonder why Trish had wanted to talk to me.

"It's just that I know Marcus very well," she continued. "And it's clear to me that he's developing a crush on you."

I couldn't suppress the smile that spread across my face. Trish obviously saw my expression, but interestingly, she didn't seem pleased. I would have thought she'd be glad that if Marcus had a crush on me, that I might feel the same. Then I realized why she must be unhappy. Here I was, widowed (at least as far as she knew) and pregnant. Why would she want her son, who held so much promise, saddled with me and my problems? Problems that were actually a lot bigger than she imagined.

The smile on my face faded as it became clear to me just how unattractive I would look to Trish as a potential girlfriend to her son.

Trish had watched without comment as the emotions played across my face.

"You must be wondering why I'm getting involved," she finally said.

I didn't respond, shocked by the deep disappointment I felt, now that I realized Trish was going to tell me to discourage Marcus' interest.

"First let me say that my concern is not only for Marcus. Kate, you have a lot on your plate right now. I'm keeping you in mind as well."

I nodded, pretending to believe that my welfare played into her concerns at all.

"Let me be perfectly honest with you, Kate. Marcus has had some serious heartbreak in the past. Watching him suffer broke my heart as well. I just don't want to see him hurt like that again."

I had absolutely no idea how to respond. Didn't she know that heartbreak was a part of life and that no one was immune? I felt like I'd had more than my share, but I didn't think that would keep me from taking chances in the future.

Then I thought, why does she think getting involved with me would lead to heartbreak? But when I thought about it, I knew she was right. How could there be any other outcome except heartbreak? A relationship with me was a dead-end. I was already married. And the likelihood of Trevor agreeing to a divorce was remote. "I understand," I said softly.

Trish nodded, then stood. "I'm sure everything will work out for the best."

I followed her to the door.

With her hand on the door knob, she turned back to me. "I'd appreciate it if you didn't mention our little chat to Marcus."

"Of course," I assured her.

That evening Marcus came over to tell me about his first day at his new job. As he described how things went, who he'd met, and what tasks he'd performed, I tried to listen. But I found myself feeling detached, like I was observing the two of us together. I saw the enthusiasm on his face and heard the excitement in his voice, but I couldn't tell how he felt about me.

I knew I felt drawn to him, but I squashed the feeling down until it was a vague feeling. The only problem was, the feeling would flare up in a burst of heat at the most unexpected moments, taking me by surprise. Like when he looked at me intently with his incredible green eyes, or when a particularly brilliant smile lit up his face. Then I would find myself trying to catch my breath, though I didn't know if he noticed what was happening to me. He was too caught up in telling me the details of his day.

Finally he finished his narration and asked me about my day. At that moment I had been able to mostly douse the flame of my attraction and was able to speak with the warmth of friendship. "Same old thing for me, but it sounds like you're getting off to a great start with your new job."

"Yeah, I really like it."

"I'm happy for you."

"I have an idea," he said. "Let's go out on Friday night. You know, to celebrate the end of my first week."

After the conversation I'd had with Trish, I really wanted to turn him down. I didn't want to be responsible for his heartache. But what excuse could I give without making it sound like I didn't want to go out with him? "Sure. That sounds like fun." I would cancel our date at the last minute so he wouldn't suspect that I had planned to cancel it all along.

Chapter Twenty-Two

As soon as I got home from work on Friday I called the cell number Marcus had given me. When he answered I could tell he was busy—he sounded distracted. "I'm sorry to bother you at work, Marcus, but I wanted to give you a chance to make other plans for tonight."

"What do you mean?"

"Well, I'm really sorry to do this to you, but I'm going to have to cancel dinner tonight." I had a tiny bit of hope that he wouldn't ask why.

"Why?"

So much for my hopes. "I think I'm coming down with something," I lied. "It might be the flu."

"That's too bad. I hope you feel better."

"Thanks, Marcus. I'll talk to you later."

That was easier than I thought it would be, I thought as I hung up. Then I settled onto the couch, my laptop in front of me. Like usual, the first place I went was to my email account. And like usual, there was an email from Trevor. Sighing, I clicked it open and read his message.

Lily,

Why are you talking about divorce? We've only been married a few months. The first year of a marriage is always hard. You need to give our marriage a chance. I know I've made mistakes, but I've learned from them. Please tell me where you are. I need to see you so we can talk.

I love you with all my heart.

Trevor

I reread his email and sighed again. Was he right? Had I been too hasty in giving up? I recalled the time we'd been together after we'd gotten married. Yes, we'd both made mistakes, but ultimately he was the one who had locked me into our home. I knew I was right in asking for a divorce. I clicked Reply.

Trevor,

I'm not going to change my mind about wanting a divorce. Please don't email me again until you're ready to discuss the steps we need to take to legally end our marriage. If you send me more emails, I won't be responding to them unless you're willing to talk about a divorce.

Lily

I hit Send, then shut down my computer and turned on the TV. I felt myself getting drowsy and must have fallen asleep because the next thing I knew, someone was knocking on my front door. Glancing at the time, I saw it was nearly seven o'clock. Feeling groggy, I pushed myself off of the couch and after looking through the peephole, opened the door. Marcus stood on my porch, a broad smile on his face and a medium-size pot in his hands.

"Marcus," I said, baffled to see him there.

"Are you feeling any better?" he asked.

Oh yeah, I thought, my grogginess fading, I'm supposed to be sick. "Uh, yeah. A little." I paused. "What are you doing here? You don't want to catch what I have."

"I'm not worried," he said, then held out the pot. "I brought you some chicken soup."

"Oh, wow. That was really thoughtful of you." Shame swept over me as I thought about how nice he was being to me even though I'd broken our date by lying to him.

"Can I come in?"

Torn between wanting to spend time with him and wanting to keep him at arm's length, my desire to spend time with him won out. "Sure." I held the door open for him.

He walked straight into the kitchen and set the pot on the counter. Then he reached for a cupboard. "Where do you keep your bowls?"

"In that one," I said, pointing to one of the upper cabinets.

He took out two bowls, then opened a drawer and pulled out a pair of spoons along with a ladle. "I hope you're hungry." He glanced my way as he began ladling soup into both bowls.

"Actually I am." Since I'd just woken up from a nap, I wondered if I looked rumpled. It wouldn't be bad if I did—it would add authenticity to my lie.

"Good. You go and sit down and I'll bring the food to you."

I walked over to the dining room table and sat like an obedient child.

He slid the bowl in front of me. "There you go." Then he placed the other bowl across from me and sat in front of it. "I'm sorry I didn't bring any rolls or crackers or anything."

"Oh Marcus. Don't feel bad. Just bringing the soup was more than I ever expected."

He smiled, obviously pleased with my response.

I picked up my spoon and began eating the hot soup. There were chunks of chicken and carrots, along with noodles. "This is really good. Is it homemade?"

His grin widened. "Yes."

By his response, I wondered if he was the one who'd made it. "Did you make it?"

"I sure did."

"But when did you have time?"

"I have to admit that when you called I was really disappointed. I'd been looking forward to taking you out. Then I decided there was no reason we still couldn't eat together. I hurried home after work and put this together."

Feeling worse with every word he spoke, I decided right then that

I wouldn't break any more dates unless I had a really good reason. And his mother being afraid of his heart getting broken didn't count as a good reason. "Well, it's delicious. I had no idea you were such a good cook."

His eyes sparkled at the compliment and I wondered why I would let his mother's concerns keep me from spending time with him. Besides the fact that he was gorgeous, he was really sweet. Even so, I was afraid to give my heart too freely. After having my trust betrayed by Trevor, I was extremely hesitant to trust completely again.

But even more important, I already had a husband. I couldn't forget that fact. As much as I wanted to leave Lily behind and just be Kate, in reality, I was Lily. I hated having two personas. I felt like a fake all the time, like I had to watch every word I uttered. If I slipped up, it could mean that Trevor would be able to find me. In his emails he'd expressed nothing but love, but he had killed my trust in him and I couldn't help but wonder if he had some sort of ulterior motive.

"You're deep in thought, Kate. What's on your mind?"

I'm just thinking about my estranged and *living* husband and what he might do to me if he finds me, I thought. Out loud I said, "Nothing in particular. So tell me about your week. Do you still like your job?"

"Yeah, I really do. The people I work with are great and I'm learning so much."

I listened as he talked about his job for a while. I had finished my soup and stood to clear my dishes.

Marcus jumped up. "Here, Kate. Let me do that." He took my dishes from me and loaded the dishwasher. When he was done, he stood by the counter. "I should probably go. I'm sure you're tired."

I didn't want him to leave. "You know, I'm feeling so much better. I think I'm over whatever was bothering me before."

"Really? That's great."

"Do you want to watch a movie on my TV or something?"

"Sure. That sounds like fun."

We walked into the living room. I sat on the couch first and Marcus sat next to me, but not close enough that we were touching. I handed him the remote. "Here, you can pick what we watch."

"Okay." He turned on the TV and began channel surfing until he found a movie that was starting. "Is this one okay?"

Not caring what we watched, I told him it was fine. I tucked my feet under me, which made me tilt in his direction. After a moment, he put his arm around me. I hadn't had much in the way of human touch in the last few weeks and I found myself leaning against him ever so slightly. When his arm tightened around me, pulling me closer, heat rushed through me. It felt so good to have him close, I never wanted to move.

After a little while I realized I desperately needed to use the bathroom. Being pregnant made me need to go more often, and I hadn't gone since before my nap, several hours earlier. Afraid that if I got up he would think I didn't want his arm around me, I hesitated. Finally, my body's needs were too powerful to ignore.

"I'll be right back," I said, setting my feet on the floor and pushing myself to a standing position. I ran upstairs to use the bathroom, then came back down and sat on the couch where I had been sitting before. Marcus immediately put his arm back around me and I snuggled up against his side.

An hour later the movie ended. Marcus unwrapped his arm from around my shoulder and slid forward so that he was on the edge of the couch, ready to stand up.

"I should let you get some rest, Kate."

Even though I was very attracted to him, I wasn't going to be the one who would initiate a kiss. And even though I had left Trevor, I was still legally married to him and it felt wrong for me to be the aggressor in this relationship. In fact, I wasn't entirely comfortable with the idea of kissing Marcus at all. Though I badly wanted to, something inside of me prevented me from actively pursuing a kiss. "Thanks for bringing the soup. You're very thoughtful, Marcus."

Still sitting on the couch, he gazed at me. "You're worth it," he said.

His incredible green eyes drew me in and my desire to kiss him grew. But I waited for him to make the first move. Suddenly he glanced away and the moment was gone. I wondered why he was so hesitant to kiss me. Was he actually afraid of heartbreak, like his mother had warned me? Or was it something else? Could he sense that I really wasn't who I said I was?

He stood and I stood as well.

"If you're still interested, Kate, I can show you some of those hand-to-hand combat moves that I told you about."

Besides the fact that I did want to learn those moves, I also knew it would be a good reason to spend time with him. "Yeah, I'd like that."

"How about tomorrow?"

"I have to work in the morning, but I'll be home a little after one."

He grinned. "Great. I'll come by about two o'clock."

We walked toward the door. "I'll see you tomorrow," he said, before opening the door and walking onto the porch.

"Bye, Marcus."

I locked the door behind him and went to bed, thoughts of Marcus filling my head.

CHAPTER TWENTY-THREE

At two-fifteen on Saturday afternoon Marcus knocked on my door. When I opened it I saw that he was wearing sweats, just like me. After coming in, Marcus asked where I wanted to have our lesson.

"It's not too hot today. How about out back?"

"Works for me," he said.

I led him to the backyard, where Greta was lying in the sun. At Marcus' arrival, she trotted over to him looking for attention.

"Hey, Greta," he said, squatting down and giving her a scratch. After a moment he stood and walked onto the grass. "All right, Kate. Are you ready to get started?"

"I think so." I walked to where he stood, then told Greta to stay on the porch, which she miraculously did. As I approached Marcus, I noticed him glancing at my belly.

"I have to admit, I'm a little nervous. I don't want to do anything that might hurt your baby," he said.

"We can just go slow. I'm sure it will be fine. Everything was okay in my self-defense class."

"Okay. If you're sure."

"I am."

"Okay. If someone steps toward you like this," he said, while moving toward me suddenly. "And grabs you like this." He reached toward me in a threatening motion and I jumped back, startled.

Suddenly I heard a low growling sound, then loud barking. I looked at Greta who stood on the porch, her teeth bared and her eyes locked on Marcus. Hurrying over to calm her, I hugged her and told her it was okay.

"Wow. I don't know if you need this training as long as you have her around," Marcus said.

"Come over here and let her know you didn't mean to threaten me," I said, motioning for him to approach Greta, who had settled down.

Marcus stepped in our direction and Greta immediately warned him with another growl and more barking.

"It's okay, Greta," I soothed. "Marcus is our friend."

When Marcus got close, he held out his hand for Greta to sniff, while I held her collar and murmured to her. Greta sniffed Marcus' hand, then began licking it. He got closer, then gave her a good scratch.

"It looks like you're friends again," I said. "Maybe I'd better lock her in the house for the rest of the lesson."

"That's probably a good idea."

I led Greta into the house, slid the plastic cover into the dog door to prevent her from coming through, then went back outside. She barked a few times, unhappy to be kept away from the action, but finally stopped. I hoped she would decide to lay down on her pet bed.

"Okay. Where were we?" Marcus asked as he went back onto the grass.

I followed him over. We stepped through several moves and I tried to focus on what he was teaching me and not get distracted by his closeness. We went through the movements slowly, Marcus obviously concerned about my baby.

"Okay," Marcus said, stepping back. "I want to try something different. I want you to be the aggressor and I'll be the defender. It's helpful for you to try out both sides to really get a feel for everything."

I nodded. "Okay."

"You step toward me and try to strike me like I did with you before."

I stepped toward him and swung my right fist upward toward his chin. Since he was a head taller than me, it didn't feel like I was being effective. As my fist approached his body, he blocked it easily. I tried with my left fist and then with my right again, but he blocked each attempt.

Dropping my arms to my sides in frustration, I watched as he relaxed, probably ready to console me. Without any warning, I swung my closed fist into his stomach. It was like hitting a brick wall. "Ow!" I said, surprised.

He laughed. "Why are you saying ouch? You're the one who hit me."

I laughed, too. "I got you though."

"Yeah, you did. Good job."

"Not that it did any damage. I don't know how effective I'd be if I actually had to defend myself." Even though Trevor wasn't quite as tall as Marcus, he was in good shape and was certainly stronger than me.

"You just need more practice, Kate. It's really not about who's bigger or stronger, but more about knowing the right places to strike."

"I hope you're right."

"I don't know about you, but I think it's getting pretty hot out here. I think we should call it good for today."

"Okay. But I feel like I could use more practice. Do you think we can do this again?"

"Sure. How about tomorrow morning?"

"Yeah, that works," I said.

We agreed on a time that worked for both of us.

"I promised my mom I would take care of some projects around the house, so I need to get going," he said.

"Okay. I'll see you in the morning."

I watched as he went out through the gate. I had enjoyed our time together and was beginning to feel a little more confident in my ability to defend myself, although I knew I had a long way to go.

Chapter Twenty-Four

Mid-morning the next day Marcus came over. Before we went out to the backyard, I dropped the plastic shield into the dog door to keep Greta inside.

"I've been thinking about today's lesson, Kate, and I think it would be more beneficial to you if we focused on defense. So today I just want you to practice breaking away from me and then disabling me."

"That sounds good," I said, following him out back.

He stopped on the porch and turned toward me. "Okay. Let's do the choke hold."

Marcus stepped toward me and put his hands around my throat.

"How would you get out of this?" he asked.

I did the moves Steve had taught me in my self-defense class and was able to break out of his grip.

He smiled. "Very good. Do you know how to disable me so that you can get away?"

"Yeah. My self-defense instructor showed me how."

"Okay. Let's do it again. Only this time do the moves that would disable me."

"All right."

We went through the movements and Marcus seemed pleased with what I could do. We practiced a few more times and I really felt like it was becoming second nature.

"Now let's work on what you would do if someone came up behind you and grabbed you," Marcus said as he walked onto the grass.

I followed him, then turned my back.

"I don't want you to know exactly when I'm going to attack, but I know you'll still be expecting it. Of course in real life you won't be expecting it at all, but I'll do my best to surprise you."

My heart pounded as I waited for him to attack. A mixture of fear and anticipation rushed through me. I could feel my adrenaline pumping as I mentally prepared for him to grab me, but I also felt excitement at the prospect of having his arms around me. Day by day, my loneliness had increased and I yearned for the touch of another person. Though Marcus and I had been touching each other through our lessons, they'd all been relatively brief and I had been focused on getting it right. Now that I was feeling more comfortable with the various moves, I was able to think about Marcus' closeness.

As my mind wandered, I lost focus on what was about to happen. Marcus must have noticed my body relaxing, because that was when he struck. I gasped in surprise as his arms wrapped tightly around me and my arms were disabled. After about a second, I gathered my wits and reacted, going through the motions I'd learned. In less than five seconds I was free and Marcus was disabled. I hadn't actually hurt him, but had gone through the motions.

He grinned. "That was very good, Kate."

I smiled back, proud I had done well. "Thanks."

"Do you want to try it again?"

I agreed and we did it again several times and each time I became more confident.

"I think you've got it down," he said.

"Thanks for teaching me all of this, Marcus."

"You've been a very good student."

I heard Greta barking. "I think someone wants to join us." After letting Greta out, I came back and sat next to Marcus, who was sitting on the porch steps.

"You sure have been serious about this whole self-defense thing,

Kate. I know you said it's because you live alone, but are you sure it isn't because you have some stalker you're worried about?"

He smiled when he said it, but he didn't know how true his statement was. I forced a laugh. "Come on now, Marcus. That's just crazy. Don't you think it's just a good idea for women to know how to protect themselves?"

"Oh, absolutely. I was just wondering."

I got up and grabbed Greta's ball, then threw it for her. She chased it down and brought it back to me, dropping it at my feet. "So, what else do you have planned today?" I asked as I threw the ball again.

"I just need to finish up the projects I started yesterday. What about you?"

"Run a few errands. Pull weeds. Stuff like that."

"Sounds like we both have very exciting days planned."

I laughed. "Well, my life just isn't very exciting. But I like it that way."

"Yeah. Keep it simple, right?"

"Yep," I said as Greta chased after the ball again.

"If you'd like, I can help you pull weeds for a while."

"I wasn't hinting," I said as I turned toward him. "You don't have to help. That's one thing I can do myself."

"No, I want to help."

"Are you sure?"

"Yeah," he said, as he stood. "Where do you keep your gardening tools?"

"I'm not that fancy," I laughed. "I just have a pair of gloves and that bucket over there." I pointed to a five gallon bucket sitting in a corner of the porch.

"That'll work."

"Before we start, let me make us something cold to drink."

"Okay. While you do that, I'm going to run home and grab a pair of gloves."

When he left, I went into the kitchen and began making lemonade. As I stirred the yellow liquid, Marcus knocked on the back door.

"Come in," I said. "I'm almost done."

He had a funny look on his face.

"What's wrong?" I asked.

"I'm really sorry, Kate. It looks like I'll have to help you pull weeds another time. My mom needs me to take care of some things for her."

"I see how it is," I joked. "Trying to get out of the hard work."

"Yeah. Now you're getting to know the real me," he said, grinning.

A thought occurred to me. "Did your mom know you were here?"

A quizzical look crossed his face. "Actually, no. And she was kind of mad that she couldn't find me. I had left my cell phone at home."

"Well, thanks for offering anyway. I can guarantee there will be weeds to pull the next time you're in the mood."

"Okay. See you later, Kate."

As I sipped my lemonade, I thought about Trish and our recent conversation. Was she now actively trying to keep Marcus from spending time with me?

CHAPTER TWENTY-FIVE

Over the next two weeks I didn't hear from Marcus at all. Surprisingly, I didn't hear from Trevor either, which was nice. I kept busy most mornings working at *Billi's* boutique and in the afternoons I frequently took long naps.

One afternoon, as I entered my sixteenth week of pregnancy, I woke with a start. At first I wasn't sure what woke me and I listened carefully, but all I heard was the sound of the air conditioner, which seemed to run constantly. Trish hadn't been exaggerating when she said how hot it got in the summer.

I closed my eyes, my head on the pillow, and tried to fall back asleep. My eyes shot open as I felt fluttering in my womb. I could feel my baby moving! That's what had woken me.

"Greta! I felt the baby!"

Greta, who was lying on her pet bed, lifted her head and her tail started wagging.

I placed my hands on my abdomen. I couldn't feel anything with my hands, but inside I could feel a slight flutter that I was certain was the baby moving. My heart swelled with love as I pictured my little baby moving around inside me. I wondered if it was a boy or a girl. I had an appointment with the doctor later in the week, and then I would make an appointment for my twenty-week ultrasound.

That evening after dinner, as I was relaxing with a book, Marcus stopped by. After not hearing anything from him for the previous two weeks, I was kind of surprised to see him on my front porch.

"Hi, Marcus. How have you been?" I asked, happy to see him. "Come in."

"Good. Work's been keeping me busy though," he said as he followed me into the living room.

"I hope you're still enjoying your job." I sat on the couch and Marcus sat near me.

"I am, but it hasn't been leaving me much free time. I'm a little worried about school in the fall. I've signed up for evening classes, but I'm nervous about how I'll fit in homework."

I thought about my own fall schedule. I would work in the mornings and attend classes in the afternoons. It would be busy, but at least I only worked part-time. "I'm sure you'll make it work," I said.

He smiled. "Are you always so optimistic?"

"I try to be."

"Kate, the reason I stopped by was to see if you wanted to go to dinner with me on Friday night."

"Oh." I wondered what Trish would think about this. I could only assume she didn't know. But Marcus and I were adults. We could go to dinner if we chose to. "Sure. I'd love to."

His ever present grin widened. "Awesome. I'll pick you up about six."

He stayed a while longer. When he left, the emptiness of my house seemed more apparent than before, but I knew that soon I would have a little one around to keep me busy. I smiled at the thought.

On Friday night, as Marcus and I drove to the restaurant, he told me about his work week. He had asked about my days too, but I didn't want to talk about my job and I encouraged him to talk about his.

"It looks like I'll have the opportunity to travel once in a while, which would be really exciting."

"Sounds like fun. Do you know if you'll be going anywhere soon?'

"I'll probably go somewhere next month. It's not for sure yet though," he said as he pulled into a parking space.

After he opened the door for me and led me inside, we were taken to a table. After we ordered, there was a lull in the conversation and I decided to ask a question that had been in the back of my mind.

"So, Marcus," I started.

"Yes, Kate?" he asked, smiling.

"Can I ask you a personal question?"

"I guess so. But I can't promise I'll answer."

"Fair enough." I paused. "I was just wondering why you don't have a girlfriend." When he didn't respond, I tried to fill the silence. "I mean, you're a great guy and everything, so I was just wondering."

"And everything?" he asked, a twinkle in his eyes.

"Now you're just fishing for compliments."

"I actually had a girlfriend not too long ago."

"Had?"

He picked up his water glass and took a drink. "We broke up."

I nodded, hoping he would give me more information. Since Trish had told me he'd had his heart broken, coupled with the fact that he seemed to like me but had never tried to kiss me, I had become curious about exactly what had happened.

"How long ago was this?" I asked.

"You don't really want to hear about my boring love life, do you?"

"Actually, I *am* interested."

"Why?"

Resting my forearms on the table, I leaned forward and spoke softly, forcing Marcus to lean closer to me. "You and I have spent some time together and I think we've both enjoyed that time. I don't know if it's going to lead anywhere, but I just need to know what kind of a person I'm spending time with." As I thought about Trevor and the time I had spent with him and then the pain I'd suffered because of him, I felt tears fill my eyes. Annoyed with myself for getting emotional, I looked at my lap and blinked a few times, getting my emotions under control. When I looked back at Marcus, he looked concerned.

"Are you all right, Kate?"

I nodded. "It's just that I've been in a bad relationship and I . . ." I shook my head. "Never mind. It's none of my business." As I spoke, I realized how truly scared I was to get close to anyone. When I'd opened my heart to Trevor, he had stomped all over it. I realized now how terrified I was that that would happen again.

"Look, Kate. I don't really want to get into the details of my past relationships. Suffice it to say that with betrayal comes pain."

From the way he said it, I could only assume his girlfriend had betrayed him. Obviously that experience had left him wary. I completely understood how he felt. Somehow, knowing he had experienced feelings of betrayal too made me feel closer to him.

"You know, I think we understand each other," I said, smiling tentatively. "We've both been hurt by someone we trusted. It's hard to get over."

He smiled in return. "Like I told you before, you're a special woman, Kate."

I felt my face redden and I shook my head.

"Really," he said. "You always know the right thing to say to make me feel better."

I didn't know what I'd said that had made him feel better. "Thanks."

This time when Marcus took me home we said good-night on the front porch and neither one of us seemed to feel the uncertainty of whether we should share a good-night kiss. It felt like our relationship had moved more securely into the friendship zone.

As I got ready for bed I thought about where our relationship was going and wasn't sure if I liked it or not. The friendship was certainly more comfortable than a boyfriend/girlfriend relationship would be, but I found myself going back and forth between wanting to just remain friends and wanting more.

CHAPTER TWENTY-SIX

The next time I checked my email, I found a message from Trevor.

Lily,

I've thought about it and I've decided I'll consider a divorce. But you need to do one small thing first. You need to send me back my gym bag. Once I receive it, I'll move ahead with the divorce. I'm not happy about this, but I'm doing it because I love you enough to let you go.

Love,

Trevor

I pictured the gym bag he was talking about. It was where he'd put the money he'd stolen from me. I'd found it in his locker at Rob's Auto Body shop. And now it was in a box somewhere in my secret room.

I pressed Reply.

Trevor,

Of course I'll send you the gym bag.

Then I stopped. If I sent a package, he'd see where I'd sent it from and he'd be able to find me. I pressed the backspace key until the reply disappeared. Then I started typing again.

Trevor,

How stupid do you think I am? I'm not going to do anything that will help you find me. Can't you see that it is over for us? Why won't you just accept that?

Lily

I pressed Send and sat back with a sigh.

I received Trevor's reply later that day.

Lily,

I'm having a hard time believing there is no hope for us. When I think about our wedding day and how much we loved each other, I believe we can still make our marriage work. Please tell me where you are, Lily. I miss you so much. I've been so lonely without you. My arms ache to hold you. I love you with all my heart.

Love,

Trevor

As I reread his email, I realized tears were trailing down my cheeks. I couldn't help it. Though I believed our marriage was over, I mourned for the loss of the happy moments. Not only that, but I had been feeling more lonely too. Since Marcus and I had settled into a friendship relationship, I couldn't help but miss the physical closeness Trevor and I had shared.

I read his email once more and was tempted to tell him where I was. I imagined him showing up at my door and instead of the frightening encounter I had prepared for, I visualized his beautiful smile and striking blue eyes as his face lit up with happiness in seeing me. I pictured Trevor by my side as I gave birth to our child, the three of us forming an idyllic family.

The more I thought about it, the more I wanted it. Trevor was still my husband. It was right and good for me to want to be with him.

It wasn't so bad at the end, I thought. Yes, I couldn't leave when I wanted, but Trevor treated me okay. He took care of me. He only had my needs in mind.

Then, as if coming out of a trance, I shook my head. What was I thinking? He had imprisoned me and isolated me. He never wanted to let me go. I had no freedom. And he had physically hurt me several times.

But had he changed? All of his recent emails had been so full of love. Was he pretending or had he actually changed? I wondered how he would respond if I purposely tried to provoke him.

Trevor,

I don't think you mean what you say. I think you're trying to manipulate me. After the way you treated me, lying to me, stealing from me, I will NEVER be able to trust you again. It is over! Know this - I will NEVER want to be with you again. I deserve better and you don't deserve to be with me or with our child.

Lily

My finger hovered over the mouse. Guilt at my harsh words flowed through me. I had never purposely tried to hurt someone like that before. If he really had changed, my words would cut him to the core. But if he was just pretending, he deserved every word.

Finally I pressed Send, then shut down my computer and went outside to play with Greta.

When Trevor replied, his tone was definitely unfriendly. But I didn't know if that was because I'd hurt him and he wanted to hurt me back or because he truly believed the things he said.

As I reread the email, I almost felt physical pain at the words he said.

Lily,

I don't know where you get off saying those things to me, but what makes you think you deserve to be the mother of my child? All I can say is that you'd better put my name on the baby's birth certificate. The baby is mine as much as yours. In fact, I believe I'll be a much better parent than you would ever be. How would you even know how to be a mother? Your mother died when you were little, so you don't even know what being a mother is all about. But my mother is still alive. How dare you think you can keep my child away from its father and grandparents, aunts, uncles, and cousins. If the baby is with you, you will be depriving him or her of having a real family.

You're selfish! You think only of yourself. A real mother would put her child before herself. Just more proof that you will never be a real mother!

I sobbed as his words sunk into my heart. He had voiced every doubt I had about my ability to be a good mother to my child. The tears flowed unabated and I did nothing to stop them, allowing all my worries and fears to be laid bare.

When I finally felt myself winding down, I went into the bathroom and looked in the mirror. My eyes were red and swollen. I splashed cold water on my face and patted it dry. Greta pressed against me, apparently sensing how upset I was. I reached down and pet her.

"Let's go play," I said, thinking I would feel better if I went outdoors in the warm sun and played with my sweet dog.

She followed me out back and we began her favorite game—fetch. After a few minutes I heard a familiar voice calling my name. I looked toward the gate and saw Marcus coming through.

Oh no, I thought. He'll probably be able to tell I was crying.

Still a safe distance away, I called hello then turned my back and threw the ball for Greta.

"Hi, Kate," he said as he approached.

"How are you, Marcus?" I kept my face mostly turned away—enough so that he couldn't see my red eyes, but not so much as to arouse suspicion.

"I'm doing great. How about you?" he said.

"I'm fine. So what's new?" Greta dropped the ball at my feet. I picked it up and threw it again. This time, after she captured the ball, she took it with her into the bushes as she followed a scent that apparently caught her attention. I stood staring at her.

"Kate," Marcus said, obviously trying to get my attention.

"Yeah?" I said, not turning toward him. Why didn't I think to put on sunglasses, I thought.

"Kate, look at me."

Slowly, I turned toward him and hoped he wouldn't notice my red eyes.

"Were you crying?" he asked.

I shook my head. "I don't want to talk about it."

His voice softened. "What's wrong, Kate?"

The empathy he clearly felt made my tender feelings rush forward and fresh tears pushed their way into my eyes. He obviously saw them too.

He pulled me into his arms. "Oh, Kate. It's all right. Whatever it is, it will be all right."

I felt so safe and secure in his arms that I could almost believe him.

He held me like that for a full minute. Finally, when I'd gotten myself under control, I pulled back slightly and looked at his face. I tried to laugh it off.

"I'm sorry about that, Marcus. Pregnancy hormones I guess."

He smiled down at me, and with one finger he gently wiped away a tear that hovered near my eye. His other arm was still wrapped around my shoulders and our bodies were nearly touching. My eyes locked on his as his free hand traced my jawline, then stopped under my chin.

I watched his face move closer to mine and my pulse skyrocketed in anticipation. When his eyes began to close, I closed mine as well. After what seemed an eternity, his lips met mine. Fire ignited throughout my body and I eagerly kissed him back.

The hand that was under my chin moved to wrap around my waist and my arms snaked around his neck. His tongue pushed into my mouth and I responded with urgency. After a long moment we pulled apart, both of us breathless.

I gazed into his eyes and his face broke into a wide grin. His happiness was contagious and I smiled back. Though my eyes still felt swollen, the words that had caused those tears faded to the back of my mind. My focus had shifted to the man standing in front of me.

"Not sure where that came from," Marcus said as he released me.

My emotions were in an uproar, having been crushed earlier and then soaring when Marcus kissed me. I could feel my emotions sinking as I wondered if he regretted the kiss we'd shared. I wasn't sure how to respond to his comment. If he regretted the kiss and wanted to keep our relationship platonic, I didn't want him to know that I definitely had more than a friendly feeling toward him now.

Greta appeared at my side and demanded my attention. Grateful for the distraction, I squatted next to her and scratched her back and her tail wagged in pleasure. After a few moments something caught her eye and she scampered off. Standing slowly, I faced Marcus. His eyes were on me and he seemed to be holding back a smile.

"What are you smiling about?" I asked, trying to gauge how he felt about our kiss.

"Me? I wasn't smiling."

"Okay. Whatever you say."

"Do you want to tell me now what made you so upset?"

Obviously, he wasn't going to do or say anything to clarify his feelings for me.

"It was nothing, Marcus. Just pregnancy hormones getting the best of me."

"If you say so. But I hope you know I'm always available if you need someone to talk to."

"Thanks, Marcus. That's nice to know." I paused then asked, "So what brought you over here today?"

"Oh yeah." He reached into his back pocket and pulled out a pair of leather gloves. "I came to see if you needed help pulling weeds."

I laughed. "Really?"

"Yes, really."

"Okay. Let's get started then."

Marcus got the bucket from the porch and brought it over to a weedy part of the yard. He knelt on the grass and began pulling weeds, then dropping them into the bucket. He stopped and looked at me, his ever-present smile on his face. "Aren't you going to pull weeds too?"

I laughed again. "I don't know what gave you that idea. I just came out here to play with my dog."

He turned back to the task. "Okay fine. Leave the real work to me."

"That's what friends are for," I said.

He turned and looked at me again, a slow smile spreading across his face. "Whatever you say, Kate." Then he turned back to the weeds.

His response left me as confused as ever. Did he still want to just be friends or did he want to take it up a notch? I considered asking him straight out, but I wasn't brave enough. If he said he just wanted to be friends, I feared I would plunge into a feeling of sadness, all hope crushed. But if he said he was ready to take it to the next level, I would be tormented with guilt over the fact that I was still married and Marcus had no idea, which could end up crushing his heart. I didn't want to do that to him.

It was better not to know, I decided. Sighing, I went and got my gloves and knelt next to him on the grass.

"So you will do the hard work, huh?" he said.

"I've always done the hard work, so you'd better watch it," I said as I gently shoved his arm.

"Or what?" He said, turning to face me.

"Or I won't let you come over and help me anymore."

He laughed. "That would show me, wouldn't it?"

"That depends."

"On?"

"Whether or not you like coming over."

The smile left his face and his eyes seemed to soften. "I do like coming over, Kate."

The tension increased and I felt certain he was going to kiss me again. Suddenly Greta nosed her way between us and the moment was lost.

Marcus put his arm around her. "Greta, what are you up to?" He rubbed her side and I found myself longing to have his strong arms wrapped securely around me.

Greta went off again and we pulled weeds for a while in a companionable silence. The ringing of Marcus' cell phone broke the quiet. After a brief conversation he hung up then turned to me.

"I need to take off, Kate." He stood.

I stayed kneeling on the grass. "Okay. Thanks for your help."

"I hope you'll let me come back," he said with a sparkle in his eyes.

"I guess that would be okay," I said, smiling.

"All right. I'll see you later then."

He left through the gate and as I watched him go, I admitted to myself that even though it would make me feel guilty, I wanted to be more than friends with Marcus. The question was, did he feel the same?

Chapter Twenty-Seven

Later that evening I forced myself to reread the email from Trevor. It hurt just as much as it had the first time I'd read it. I tried to convince myself that he was only saying those things because of the hurtful words I'd sent him before.

I debated whether I should bother replying. What purpose would that serve? But after I'd admitted to myself how attracted I was to Marcus, I felt more urgency to be able to get on with my life. As long as I was married to Trevor, I was in a kind of limbo and I would never be able to fully give of myself to anyone.

Trevor,

I'm sorry you feel that I would be a horrible mother to our child, because I am the only mother our child will have. I'm sure I'll make mistakes, but that's part of life. I'm also sorry about the things I said to you in my last email. That was mean and uncalled for. Please accept my apology.

Don't you think, for our baby's sake, that it would be best if you and I can be friends? Even if we can't be together as husband and wife, we need to be able to work together to raise our child.

Do you think that's possible?

Lily

This time he replied almost instantly. It almost made me feel like he was right there next to me. I didn't like that feeling.

Lily,

Okay, I guess I'm sorry too. But how can you go on and on about us working together to raise our child when I don't even know where you are?

How does that even work? It looks like it is up to you now to show how serious you are about this. We need to meet, face to face, to talk about everything. Then I'll know you're serious.

Trevor

The idea of being in the same room as him scared me deeply. He had so much anger inside, there was no telling what would set him off. Just like in his emails. He'd been all loving and sweet, then bam, he started saying all kinds of horrible things.

Trevor,

I'm not ready to meet with you yet. But we both need to be able to get on with our lives. We need to legally end our marriage. Will you cooperate in a divorce?

Lily

Again, he responded immediately.

Lily,

Like I told you before, if you'll send me back my gym bag, I'll cooperate in a divorce.

Let me know when you've sent it.

Trevor

If I wanted Trevor to cooperate in the divorce, I knew I would have to go along with his demand. It was really a simple thing so why should I resist? I could figure out a way to get it to him without divulging my location.

Okay Trevor. I'll let you know when the gym bag has been shipped.

Lily

He didn't reply, so I shut down my laptop and thought about how I could ship the bag to him while keeping my location a secret.

I could drive the few hours to Reno and ship from there. Then the postage would show Reno.

Feeling good about my solution, I decided to get going on it right away. I'd have to arrange for a day or two off from work, but that wouldn't be too difficult. I walked upstairs and into the baby's room, then opened the closet and then the door to the secret room. Pushing aside the blank I'd hung over the door, I crawled inside and turned on the lamp that I had put in a corner previously.

It took me a few minutes to locate the gym bag since I couldn't remember exactly which box I'd put it in. Carrying the bag downstairs, I set it on the dining room table, then went into the kitchen to make myself dinner.

At least it shouldn't cost much to ship, I thought, since it weighs next to nothing. I wonder why Trevor was being such a jerk about me sending it back to him. Yes, it was the only item of his that I'd taken, but it had held the money that *he'd* stolen from *me*.

Whatever, I thought. As long as I get what I want, what do I care that he wants this bag so much.

Wait a minute, I suddenly thought, stopping my meal preparations. Why *does* he want it so bad anyway?

I set down the vegetables I had been chopping and walked over to the table. The gym bag lay on the table, flat and empty. At least I assumed it was empty. I unzipped the main section and looked inside. It appeared empty. I felt around and didn't feel anything but seams. I zipped it closed and checked one of the side pockets. It was empty too. Flipping it over, I unzipped the only other pocket and stuck my hand in. I felt around and began pulling my hand out, but for some reason, I decided to examine the inside a little more closely. A hard crumb of some kind pressed against my finger, but then I felt something small, hard, and smooth.

Using my fingertips, I pulled out the object. It was so small it would have been very difficult to accidentally stumble upon it. I examined the object and immediately recognized it as an SD card, the kind used in digital cameras to store photos.

Was this what Trevor really wanted back?

CHAPTER TWENTY-EIGHT

After booting up my computer, I slid the SD card into the slot on the side of my laptop. A screen popped up giving me some choices and I clicked on the option to view the pictures. Another screen appeared with about twenty thumbnail photos. I clicked on the first one in the series, which enlarged it. The picture showed Rob, Trevor's boss and the owner of Rob's Auto Body shop. He was smiling and standing next to a counter at the shop. There were cars in the background, obviously in the process of being repaired, and I recognized the location as being the shop.

Rob held a beer in one hand and with the other he pointed to an open metal box which sat on the counter. The box looked like it was about the same dimensions as my laptop, which was about eighteen inches by twelve inches. The box looked like it was about six inches deep. But the most interesting aspect of the box was that it looked like it was completely filled with cash.

Most of the bills on top were twenty dollar bills. The others were varying denominations. I could only assume that money was stacked beneath the top layer.

I pressed the arrow key on my keyboard to move to the next picture. This time it was Trevor standing by the counter, but he looked like he was running his fingers through the money. The next picture showed the box closed and Rob putting a sturdy lock through the two metal loops which overlapped when the lid was closed.

The next few pictures looked like they were all taken out in the desert. They showed Trevor and Rob taking turns digging a hole, then Rob placing the metal box in the hole, then Trevor filling it in and smoothing it over.

The next one showed Trevor stacking a few rocks in the spot where the box was buried. The next one was actually a video. It showed Rob sitting in the passenger seat of Trevor's Camaro. He appeared to be passed out. I could hear Trevor's voice.

"Look at him" Trevor said, derision clear in his voice. "He's so out of it, he probably won't even remember we came out here." The video ended with Trevor's laughter.

The last photo was taken from inside the car, looking out through the windshield at the place where the box had been buried.

I went through the slide show a few more times, then tried to think why Trevor would want it back so badly that he was willing to grant me a divorce.

I mentally listed the reasons I could think of. Maybe Rob told him to get it back or is threatening him. Maybe he wants to make sure no one else sees it. But the most likely reason was that he needed the pictures to help him find where he'd buried the money. But would he be able to find it just based on these pictures? If he already had an idea where it was, I would think these pictures would be unnecessary.

Unless, I thought, a smile turning up the corners of my mouth, there is other information stored on this memory card. Quickly closing the pictures, I clicked on "My Computer", then opened the drive letter assigned to the SD card. I saw a folder where the pictures were stored, but there was also a text file on the root of the drive. I opened the file and saw two groups of numbers.

With GPS being used so commonly, I assumed these were the coordinates for where Trevor and Rob had buried the metal box full of money. And since Trevor was so anxious to get this SD card back, I could only assume that he couldn't remember where he had buried it. The money must still be where he'd put it.

"Greta, how would you like to go on a treasure hunt?"

She lifted her head from where it had been resting on her paws and began wagging her tail.

Googling the coordinates in the file, I saw that the spot was not too far outside of Reno. I didn't own a GPS unit, but wondered if Marcus had one I could borrow. But first I needed to arrange to take a couple of days off. I also needed a shovel.

I called Billi and asked if it would be possible to take the next two days off to attend to a personal matter. In all the time I'd worked there, I'd never been late or missed a day of work, so I couldn't see how she could object.

She told me she would need to check with Maddy to see if she could cover for me and she would call me back. While I waited to hear back from her, I called Marcus on his cell phone.

"Hey, Kate," he said. "What's up?"

"I was wondering if you could do me a favor."

"Not pull more weeds, I hope."

I laughed. "No. I was wondering if you have a GPS device that I could borrow for a couple of days."

"Sure. Are you going on a trip or something?"

"Yes. As a matter of fact, I am."

"When do you need it?"

"I'm hoping to leave in the morning."

"Oh. I can bring it over now if you want."

"Thanks. That would be great."

After we hung up, Billi called back and said Maddy had agreed to cover for me. I thanked her and hung up.

A few minutes later Marcus knocked on the door. I let him in and invited him to sit on the couch.

He held out the GPS device. "Have you ever used one of these before?"

"No."

He showed me how to use it and I tried it out.

"What if I had specific coordinates. How would I put those in?"

He glanced at me, a questioning look on his face, then showed me how it was done. "Where are you going anyway, Kate?"

"Just down to Vegas to visit a friend," I lied.

"You've been there before though, right?"

"Of course. It's just that I was thinking of buying one of these, but I wanted to try one out first." A lie on top of a lie. Nice. But I certainly couldn't tell him the truth. Oh yeah, Marcus. My husband, who is alive and well by the way, won't give me a divorce unless I send him back what amounts to a treasure map. But I'm going to see if I can dig up the treasure he buried before he has a chance to. Yeah, I thought. I'm sure that would go over really well.

"It's probably a good idea to try it out before you buy one. They can be kind of expensive."

I smiled. "Don't worry. I'll be careful with it."

He smiled back. "I know. I'm not worried."

I wished I could ask him if I could borrow a shovel, but that would invite too many unwelcome questions. "Well, I'm going to get an early start, so I should probably go to bed soon."

"Okay. I can take a hint." He stood. "Have a good drive. I'll see you when you get back."

I walked him to the door and said good-night, then went upstairs and began packing. I didn't know if I'd be spending the night, but I wanted to be prepared.

I set my suitcase and Greta's things by the front door then went to bed. I really did want to get an early start, even though I wasn't driving as far as Las Vegas. As I tried to visualize how the next day would go, excitement swept over me and I had trouble falling asleep.

Chapter Twenty-Nine

After stopping by a local Wal-Mart and buying a shovel, some water bottles and some snacks, I entered the freeway and headed North. I had punched in the coordinates like Marcus had shown me and followed the directions on the device.

With Greta along, I had to stop a few times to let her run around, but within four hours I was turning onto a dirt road that really did look like the middle of nowhere. When the GPS device announced that I had arrived at my destination, I smiled. But as I looked around, I didn't see the pile of rocks that Trevor had used as a marker. I wondered if they'd gotten knocked over, but I didn't see anything that resembled rocks scattered from a pile. I wondered how accurate the GPS device actually was and decided to walk around the area and see if I could find the stacked rocks.

Greta started off trotting along next to me, but soon decided to explore on her own. It was was easy to keep her within my sight since the area was mostly barren with a few small bushes here and there. I wandered around for at least thirty minutes before I came across a pile of rocks that looked familiar. I went back to my car and drove to the pile, then using my new shovel, I pushed the rocks aside and began digging. It didn't take long to reach the metal box.

I pulled it out of the hole and set it on the ground. Fortunately, it wasn't too heavy. But I would need a tool of some sort to open the lock. After setting the metal box in my trunk, I filled the hole back in and set the rocks back on top. Greta had come to see what I was doing by

155

then.

I poured some water from a water bottle into her bowl, then grabbed a fresh water bottle for myself and drank the whole thing. It was hot and I was glad the job was over. Once Greta and I were refreshed, I put the shovel in the trunk, strapped Greta into her seatbelt, and got behind the wheel.

Now that I had collected what I assumed was the cash, my next task was to ship the gym bag to Trevor. I had boxed it up, including the SD card, and addressed the package before leaving home. Now I just needed to drive to the post office and ship it. I had looked up the address of post offices in the area and punched in the address of the one I had decided to use. I followed the directions and soon found myself at the post office.

I might have to get one of these GPS devices, I thought. Especially with my bad sense of direction.

I shipped off the package, then headed west on I-80. I was back home before dinner. Though exhausted, I brought everything in. I hadn't needed my suitcase after all, but that was okay. I set the metal box in a corner of the dining room. I would need to go to the hardware store and get something to cut it with, but that would have to wait until morning.

After fixing a quick meal, I went to bed early and slept soundly all night.

I slept in the next morning since I'd taken the day off from work. The first thing I did, after getting ready for the day, was to email Trevor and let him know that I'd shipped the bag. I wondered how long it would take him to suspect me as the person who'd dug up the box. Would he think it was Rob at first? What would he do once he suspected me?

Anxious to know exactly what the box held, I drove to the hardware store as soon as I'd sent the email to Trevor.

I explained to the sales clerk that I'd lost the key to a heavy lock and I needed to get inside. Why would he doubt me, a young pregnant woman? He showed me to the bolt cutters and I bought one that I thought would work.

Driving straight home, I brought my new bolt cutters into the house, set the metal box on the kitchen counter and tried to cut the lock. After several tries, the lock snapped in two. Setting the bolt cutters on the counter, I pulled the pieces of the lock out of the metal loops and opened the lid.

Adrenaline pounded through my veins as I gazed at the money that reached the top of the box. I wanted to count it, but decided I should take it to my bedroom, just in case Marcus or anyone else stopped by. I closed the lid and carried the box up to my bedroom and set it on my bed. I ran back down to the kitchen to grab a notepad and pen, then went back up to my bedroom and began counting, writing numbers on the notepad as I grouped the money into stacks.

When I had finished, I carefully added the numbers I'd written down, then felt the blood drain from my face. Two-hundred thousand dollars. Suddenly I wished I hadn't taken it. Trevor wanted this money and I didn't know to what extremes he would go to get it back.

When he went to the GPS location and found the box was missing, he would probably suspect me right away. After all, I'd had the SD card, although he couldn't be certain I'd found it. And the postmark on the package with the gym bag would be from Reno, so it would be evident that I had recently been in Reno.

He would absolutely freak out.

Crap! Maybe I should drive back and rebury the money. But Trevor will probably receive the package today. He'll most likely go straight out to the burial spot. It's too late!

Panic engulfed me as I thought of Trevor redoubling his efforts to find me.

What had I been thinking?!

I started to shake. It felt like my blood pressure had dropped and I thought I was going to pass out. Quickly shoving the money aside, I lay on the bed for several minutes, and finally the feeling passed. I stayed on the bed, pondering what to do.

I could confess everything to Marcus and beg him to stay with me. But that wouldn't work. Not only did he have to go to work every day, but it wouldn't be fair to drag him into my problems.

I could move. But that wouldn't guarantee that Trevor wouldn't find me wherever I ended up. Plus, I was making a life for myself here. I wasn't ready to give that up yet.

Rubbing my closed eyes, I decided the only thing I could do was stash the money in my secret room and go on with my life. When I emailed Trevor about anything, I had to act as if I had no knowledge of the cash. I *could not* give myself away. And it was more imperative than ever that he not know where I was.

What effect was this going to have on Trevor granting the divorce? Would he move ahead, even though the money was gone? He couldn't come right out and blame me. Then he would be admitting the money existed, and if there was a chance I wasn't the one who took it, he wouldn't want me to know about it.

No, he wouldn't have a good excuse to delay the divorce since I'd held up my end of the bargain.

I pushed myself off of the bed, packed all the money back into the metal box, and took it into the secret room. Standing in the middle of the room, I looked around, trying to figure out the best place to hide the box. I set the metal box on the floor and then dug through some of the storage boxes to see if I could hide the metal box inside.

I finally decided on a storage box that had some space and moved things around to make room on the bottom, then placed the metal box in a bottom corner. After moving the items in the storage box around, the metal box was completely hidden. I closed the lid, then set two other storage boxes on top, but it was as if I could still feel the money there, pulling at me, taunting me, warning me.

Though I now utterly regretted digging up the money, I knew I had to live with my decision and deal with the consequences that were sure to follow.

Stupid, stupid, stupid, I screamed in my mind as I crawled out of the hidden room and into the baby's room.

CHAPTER THIRTY

As the day went on and I focused on cleaning the house, doing some laundry, and running errands, I was able to release some of the worry that had built up inside me and I began to feel better. I believed I had the upper hand in the situation with Trevor because I knew exactly what was going on, whereas he would only be able to speculate.

As I put the last of the groceries into the cupboards, I wondered if Trevor had received the package yet, and when he would drive to the burial spot and try to dig up the metal box. I decided to check my email and see if he had sent anything. After a moment I was pulling up my email account and I immediately saw an email from Trevor. As I clicked on it, my heart rate increased as I tried to guess what it would say.

Lily,

The package just arrived. Thank you for sending it. I will start the paperwork for the divorce in the morning.

Trevor

I let my breath out in a rush. I hoped he would get the paperwork going before he discovered the money was missing—although he probably wouldn't suspect me right away.

Loud knocking on the door startled me and I let out a scream. I closed the email and walked to the door, looking through the peephole. It was Marcus. Taking a deep breath to calm my racing heart, I opened the door.

"Marcus. Hi."

"Hi, Kate. How was your trip?"

"How did you know I was back?"

He motioned over his shoulder. "I saw your car out front."

"Oh, of course. Do you want to come in?"

"Sure."

He followed me inside and we sat on the couch. Then I stood. "Let me get your GPS device for you." I got it from the kitchen counter, then handed it to him. "Thanks for letting me borrow it. It was really handy to have. I think I might end up getting one."

"That was a pretty quick trip to Vegas," Marcus said. "Isn't it like an eight hour drive?"

"Uh, yeah," I stammered. "I ended up not going there. I was partway there, but, uh, my friend called and said she had to, uh, she had a family emergency, so she had to cancel. So I turned around and came back home."

"Oh. That's too bad that you had to waste all that time and gas."

"It's okay. Sometimes it's nice just to take a drive."

"Yeah, that's true," Marcus said.

"How's work going?"

"Good. But I don't want to talk about work."

"Okay. What do you want to talk about?"

Suddenly a big smile spread across his face. I smiled back, expecting him to share some good news, which I could use after the stress I'd been feeling.

"What's up, Marcus?"

"Well," he started. "Do you remember me telling you how I had recently broken up with my girlfriend?"

I remembered he had told me he'd had a girlfriend recently and that they had broken up. And with the little he'd told me, it had sounded like she had betrayed him in some way. "Yeah," I said.

"Well, last night I ran in to her and we got to talking and we decided we were going to give our relationship one more try."

I couldn't believe he was telling me this. Had he already forgotten the kiss we'd shared? Had it meant nothing to him? I thought I was going to vomit. I tried to hide my feelings, but I wasn't sure how successful I was. Hopefully he was too focused on his own happiness to notice my distress. "That's great, Marcus. I'm so happy for you." I paused. "What did you say her name was?"

"Marissa," he said, his green eyes sparkling with his good news.

"So I guess I won't be seeing much of you around here."

"I can still help you with stuff. This won't change our friendship, Kate."

I forced a laugh. "Don't you think Marissa might not like it if you spend time with me?"

He looked thoughtful. "I don't know. Maybe."

"I certainly wouldn't want to get in the way of your relationship," I said, while wondering what I could do to make sure he didn't forget about me. He was the only real friend I'd made since I'd moved here and I didn't want to lose that connection.

"You won't."

A thought occurred to me. "How does your mom feel about you getting back together with Marissa?"

Frowning, he said, "When I told her, she tried to talk me out of it. But she has to accept the fact that I'm a big boy and I can make my own decisions. In fact, now that I've got this job, I've been looking for an apartment so I can move out of my parents' house."

"Oh, well that would be good, I guess." I didn't like the idea of him not being right next door anymore. What if he moved to the next town?

"Yeah. I found a couple of places that I'm considering."

I didn't want to hear anymore of his news. It was all bad news for me. "Marcus, I have some things I have to do."

"Oh, okay." He stood.

I stood too and we walked to the door. "I hope everything works out for you."

"Thanks, Kate. Take care."

I locked the door behind him, then sat on the couch and put my face in my hands. Despair swept over me as I thought about the mess I'd made with Trevor, and now Marcus was going to be disappearing from my life. All of a sudden there didn't seem to be such a rush to get the divorce. But I still wanted to move forward with it. Who knew what was around the corner?

CHAPTER THIRTY-ONE

Over the next few weeks I didn't hear from Marcus at all and Trevor was strangely quiet as well. I considered emailing Trevor to ask how the divorce was coming along, but didn't do it because I actually wanted to avoid all contact with him. I was certain by now he had discovered the money was missing and I hoped that somehow, if he didn't talk to me, that he wouldn't even consider that I might be the one who had taken it.

Someone had finally bought Dad's house and I had deposited the proceeds in my bank account. More than ever I wished I had never found the SD card. The money sitting in the hidden room just stressed me out.

I tried to push all thoughts of Trevor and Marcus to the back of my mind and instead focused on my job, the coming of the new school year, and especially focused on my growing baby. The baby was much more active now and I was looking forward to my ultrasound. It was scheduled for later that morning and I could hardly wait.

I kept myself busy until it was time to leave for the appointment, then drove to the place where the ultrasound would be performed. I was so excited to know what I was having. Even though my main concern was to just have a healthy baby, I really was hoping for a girl.

After a short wait I was taken into an exam room. The ultrasound technician squirted some gel onto my belly and moved the wand around. As I watched the image of my baby on the screen, I was amazed by the detail.

"Do you want to know the baby's sex?" the technician asked.

"Yes," I said with enthusiasm.

She moved the wand around again. "It looks like it's a girl."

"Really? Are you sure?"

"Yes, I'm sure. Congratulations."

"Thank you," I said, thrilled to know I would be having a daughter.

On my way home I stopped by the nearby mall and bought a few pink baby outfits. I could hardly wait for her to get here.

There were only two weeks until my classes were going to start at the college. I used that time to get the baby's room finished as I knew once classes started my free time would be severely limited. I ordered a dresser and changing table online.

A few days later when I came home from work, there were two large packages on my front porch. They were too heavy for me to carry in and I knew there would probably be some assembly needed. Even though I hated to bother Marcus, I knew I would need his help to get the dresser and changing table into the baby's room.

That evening I walked over to Marcus' house and rang the doorbell. Trish answered and seemed surprised to see me.

"How are you, Kate? I haven't seen you in a while."

"I'm doing fine. Keeping busy with working."

"What can I help you with?"

"I'm sorry to bother you, but I was hoping Marcus could help me with a dresser and changing table I just had delivered."

"Oh. I thought you knew. Marcus moved out."

"No, I didn't know. But the last time I talked to him he said he was looking for a place."

"Perhaps Jeff can help you."

"That would be wonderful, if it's not too much trouble."

"I'm sure he won't mind. He should be home soon. I'll send him over when he gets home."

"No big hurry. Thanks, Trish."

As I walked back to my house, I couldn't help but feel a little sad knowing that Marcus had moved out. I wondered how much of him I would see. He'd gotten back together with Marissa and now he'd moved out. I probably wouldn't see him at all.

A little while later Marcus' dad came over and carried the furniture into the baby's room and put the changing table together. When he was done I thanked him and walked him to the door.

I was glad to get the baby's room done since I knew my time would be limited once classes started. I would still be working in the mornings and I was certain homework would take up my evenings.

Trevor had emailed me and said the divorce proceedings were under way. He had even scanned in documents and emailed them to me to prove he'd kept his word. I wondered if he suspected me in the missing money, but from the tone in his emails, it didn't seem like it. He'd been friendly, which surprised me. Maybe he had changed.

Classes started and I was excited to immerse myself in learning. One of the classes was a web design class and I was particularly excited to create a web site.

As I went to my classes I kept to myself. I decided that the fewer people I spoke to, the lower the chance that Trevor would find me. The drawback to that though, was how lonely I felt. Now that Marcus was no longer part of my life, I didn't really have any friends. I had hoped Billi and I could become friends, but when she was at the store she was either helping customers or working in her office. And my coworker, Maddy, worked afternoons, so I only saw her when she took over for me.

I longed for someone to talk to and confide in. I missed Alyssa, who had been my good friend in Reno. I'd avoided emailing her since I'd been in California for fear I'd say something that would give away where I was. But now I felt a need to talk to someone and she was the only one who had any idea about what had happened.

Alyssa,

I'm so sorry I haven't emailed you in a while. How are things for you? How are classes going? I'm going to school where I am.

Take care,

Lily

Later that week I heard back from her.

Hey, Lily!

It's so good to hear from you! I've been thinking about you. My classes are going fine this semester. I have some big news though. I'm engaged! His name is Ty and I've known him since high school. When I came back to my parents' house over the summer, we started hanging out and now we're engaged.

I've been spending every spare moment planning the wedding. My life is so crazy!

I hope you are safe and doing well. I hope I can see you sometime.

Take care of yourself,

Alyssa

Though I wanted to be able to confide in Alyssa and tell her everything that had happened, it sounded like she already had so much going on and I didn't want to burden her with my problems. I emailed her back and told her to let me know when the wedding was and if I could, I'd try to come.

As the semester went on I mostly enjoyed my classes but the web design class quickly became my favorite. I spent hours creating mock websites until I felt ready to do the real thing. One day at work I approached Billi with the idea that I could create a website for her store.

"You wouldn't have to pay me unless you liked it," I said. "Then I'll get it uploaded to the Internet and keep it updated."

"I've been thinking about getting a website for the store." Billi smiled. "Give it a try and show me what you come up with. I'm sure I'll love it."

She insisted on paying me for my time. We agreed on a price and as soon as I got home that night I began sketching the layout.

It took several weeks before I had a presentation to show Billi. Between going to school full-time, working part-time, and being exhausted all the time, I had trouble fitting this new project into my schedule.

The day I planned on showing the presentation to Billi, I brought my laptop to the boutique. When I walked into Billi's office I was caught off-guard to find several other people in the room.

"I can come back another time if you'd like," I told her.

She laughed. "Actually Kate, these are some friends of mine who own businesses of their own. I invited them to see what you've done."

"Oh." I hadn't been nervous to show my work to Billi, but this was different.

"I'm sorry, Kate. I should have warned you."

"No, that's okay."

One of the men spoke up. "I've been looking into getting a website myself, but I didn't know who to ask."

I was pleased to see everyone nod in agreement. I suddenly realized that if they liked my work, they could all become my clients. This had the potential of turning into a business for me. A business I could do and still be at home with my baby.

As the possibilities flowed through my head, my nervousness increased. This could be the most important meeting I've ever had, I thought as I booted up my laptop.

Forcing those thoughts out of my mind, I focused instead on showing Billi and the others the features I'd created. The time went quickly and I was thrilled when nearly every business person there expressed interest in my skills. Not only would I create the websites, but then I would need to maintain them as well.

I went home on a mental high as my confidence in myself and my abilities soared.

The email I found in my inbox quickly crushed those feelings.

169

Lily,

I've been thinking about you a lot lately. I've tried dating other women, but no one is like you. I NEED you. I want you to be a part of my life. I know I made some mistakes, but I've changed. I realize now how much I really love you. We were meant to be together. For me, no one else will do. It's you or no one. And I don't want to be alone. We need to be together. You, me, and our baby. I promise I'll be a good husband and father. We're still married and the divorce can be stopped. You are my wife. We need to be together. It's not fair to the baby to not be with his father. I know you want what's best for our baby.

I know you don't want to be alone. I can take care of you. I'll do anything to have us be together, Lily.

I love you!

Trevor

I was surprised to find myself crying. I didn't realize it until then just how lonely I really was. The last few months had been so difficult. Doing everything on my own had been harder than I had expected. And I hadn't even had the baby yet. How was I going to handle being a single mother? Was it really fair to my baby to keep Trevor out of her life?

As I pictured Trevor's face, I recalled the good memories. There had been so much potential for a good family life. But then I thought about the day I found out I was pregnant.

I'd prepared a special dinner and asked Trevor to come home on time from work. After promising he would, he hadn't shown up until nearly one o'clock in the morning and he had smelled strongly of alcohol. When I'd confronted him, he had shoved me so hard that I'd fallen over the coffee table and onto the floor.

As I relived that moment, I knew I couldn't live my life that way.

I hit the Reply button.

Trevor,

It's over. As much as I loved you, I can't be with you anymore. It's what's best for everyone. With your unpredictable temper, I would be afraid for our child. I'm sorry, but I believe it's for the best.

Lily

I reread the message several times, then took a deep breath and hit Send.

My hands shook as I closed the laptop.

Over the next few days I anxiously checked my email, waiting for Trevor's reply. When it came, I was almost afraid to open it. Finally, my heart pounding, I opened the message

Lily

I'm sorry you feel that way because I've changed. I know you don't believe me, but it's true. I've stopped drinking. I don't even hang out with the same people anymore. You'd be so proud of me.

Please, just give me one more chance.

I love you more than anything. Tell me where you are and I'll come and get you.

Love, Trevor

I bit my lip as I contemplated his words. Had he really changed or was he trying to trick me? I had a hard time believing he could change so completely. And the idea of him coming to get me frightened me. The last time he had done that, he'd isolated me from the world for weeks.

Chapter Thirty-Two

One day, towards the end of November, I was working at the boutique by myself. Billi was out of town and had left me in charge. I was feeling very pregnant and awkward—there were only a few weeks before my baby girl would arrive—and I was organizing some items on a shelf. The morning had been less busy than usual and there were no customers at that moment. I was enjoying the lull when I heard the bell over the front door jingle. I turned to ask the customer if I could help, but my words stuck in my throat when I saw Trevor standing there.

The blood drained from my face and panic engulfed me. Finally I found my voice and the words left my mouth without me thinking. "Trevor, you found me."

He took a step in my direction, a friendly smile on his face. "Of course I found you. Did you really think you could hide from me?"

I felt shaky and I feared I might pass out. I knew I had to do everything within my power to remain conscious and in control of myself. I moved to the chair we kept in the corner for customers, and after sitting, I lowered my head until the dizziness passed.

"Lily, are you okay?" Trevor asked as he hurried over to me.

I lifted my head and saw the genuine alarm on his face. Could it be that he really cared and wouldn't harm me? My trust in him had been shattered and I knew I couldn't take anything he said at face value.

"What are you doing here?" I choked out.

"What do you mean? I want to be with you. You're still my wife. I want to be with you and our baby."

"But Trevor, we're in the middle of a divorce."

"The divorce was your idea. I never wanted it. You left *me*, remember?"

Just then a customer came in.

"I can't do this right now," I whispered.

"That's fine. I'll wait outside until you're off. One o'clock, right?"

I nodded, still in shock to see him standing in front of me. He left and I forced myself to stand and see if the customer needed help. She said she was just looking. I turned away from her and my gaze went to the window. I could see Trevor walking across the street to a diner and realized he'd probably been watching me for a while. At least long enough to know what time I usually got off work.

It was twelve thirty, so I only had thirty minutes to devise a plan.

As I watched the customer calmly look through the clothing racks, my mind raced, frantically thinking about my options. I could call the police. But what would I tell them? My husband wants to talk to me. No officer, he hasn't threatened me and no, I don't have a restraining order, he just wants to talk to me.

No, that was a non-starter.

"Excuse me," the customer said, startling me.

"Yes?" I asked, trying to care about what she might want.

"Do you have this in a size ten?" She held up a pair of designer jeans.

"We just have what's out. I'm sorry," I said, wishing she would leave me alone so I could think.

"When are you going to get more in?"

"We get a shipment every Monday."

"Can you hold a pair of these for me in a size ten if you get some in?"

"Sure," I said, not caring that that was against store policy. I just wanted to move her along because the clock was rapidly approaching one o'clock.

"Do you want my name?" she pressed.

"Oh, yeah. Of course."

"It's Michele. That's with one l."

I went behind the counter and wrote her name. She followed me and watched—I guess to make sure I'd spelled her name right.

"Aren't you going to write down what size I need?"

"Yeah, yeah. What size was it?"

"A ten," she said, clearly becoming exasperated.

I wrote ten next to her name. "Got it."

"What about the brand of the jeans?"

"Right." I wrote that down too. At least I didn't need to ask her what she'd been looking at.

"Okay, thank you."

Mercifully, the woman left and I was able to focus. I only had ten minutes until my shift was over. Maddy would be there any minute and then I would need to leave.

I briefly considered calling Marcus, but he had moved on with his life. He was with his old girlfriend at his new job and in his new apartment. I didn't fit in that equation anywhere. Plus how was he going to feel when he found out I'd lied to him about being a widow and about my name? It didn't matter. He was out of my life.

"Hi there, Kate. Has it been busy?"

I looked up and saw Maddy walking through the door, at ease and not a care in the world. I forced myself to focus on her question. "Uh, yeah. It's been slow today."

"Are you okay? You look pale."

That's because my abusive husband tracked me down and is waiting across the street for me to come out even as we speak. "I'm not feeling very well," I said instead.

"Good thing I'm here then."

175

I nodded, my mind still racing and having no clue what to do. There was no back door in this place so I'd have to walk out the front. Maybe I could make a run for my car, I thought. But as I took a step in the direction of the front door, my big belly reminded me that my movements were slow and awkward. There would be no running today.

Resigned to dealing with Trevor face to face, I sighed.

"You'd better go home and take it easy, Kate."

"Thanks, Maddy. I'll see you tomorrow," I said as I stared out the window. At least I hoped I would be back the next day. I had no idea what Trevor was planning. How long had he been in town? Did he know where I lived? I was willing to bet two-hundred thousand dollars that he did. I would also bet that he didn't know I had his two-hundred thousand dollars. Was that why he was here? To find out if I had it? Or did he have other reasons altogether?

CHAPTER THIRTY-THREE

Maybe it would be best if I talked to him, I thought. I had no desire to keep the money. In fact I wished I'd never found the SD card. All the money was doing was stressing me out. I still had a good portion of the money I'd gotten from Dad's life insurance policy. Plus now I had the money from the sale of Dad's house. My needs were being met. I didn't need to be greedy. I'd rather have the peace of mind of knowing I was safe.

"It's okay if you want to take off," Maddy said.

It was a few minutes before one. "Okay. See ya," I said as I walked out the door, my gaze glued to the diner. I hurried to my car, wondering if I could drive off before Trevor caught up to me. I had to look away from the diner so I wouldn't trip. Walking as fast as I could in my hugely pregnant state, I reached my car and shoved the key in the lock, wishing I had a keyless entry. I turned the key and the lock popped up. My hand grasped the door handle and I pulled.

"You weren't going to leave without talking to me, were you?" Trevor said in my ear.

I gasped, startled, and dropped my keys. I considered using my self-defense moves, but didn't think I would be too effective with my big belly in the way. Not only that, I wanted to find a way to give Trevor his money back. I knew as long as I had it I would have to look over my shoulder. Maybe I could use it to get what I wanted from Trevor. Namely a divorce and a life away from him.

"You dropped these," he said, handing me my keys.

I took them from him. "What do you want to talk about?"

"Us. Our baby. But I don't want to talk to you out here in the parking lot. Why don't we go back to your place?"

Even though I was certain he already knew where I lived, I wasn't about to take him there. "I haven't had lunch yet. Why don't we go to the diner and grab a sandwich. We can talk there."

"Okay. I'll even buy your lunch," he said.

We walked across the street and into the diner and found a booth in an area where no one else was sitting. Although I'd kept to myself and hadn't gotten to know the people who regularly shopped at *Billi's*, I certainly didn't want them to overhear any of my conversation with Trevor. In fact, I would prefer if no one saw me with Trevor.

Moments after sitting, a waitress approached our table. My appetite had vanished, but I ordered a chicken salad sandwich anyway. Trevor ordered a cheeseburger, and the waitress left.

"You're looking good, Lily. I like your hair."

I touched my hair without conscious thought. I'd gotten so used to it being short that I'd forgotten that Trevor hadn't seen it that way.

"I really hope you'll allow me to feel our baby kick."

My hands went to my belly in a protective gesture, unsure if I wanted to let him touch me.

"Do you know what it is?" he asked, an eager look on his face.

Without thinking, I shook my head, then added, "No." Somehow, keeping this information to myself made the baby seem more mine than his.

"Oh," he said, obviously disappointed.

Then I thought, do I have the right to keep that information from him? After all, the baby really was his child as much as mine. But I'd already told him no. I didn't want him to know I'd lied. "How did you find me?" I finally asked.

"With the Internet it's not too hard to find someone. Especially when you have that person's social security number."

"You have my social security number? Where did you get that?"

"I'm not as stupid as you seem to think I am, Lily. Or should I say Kate?"

Of course he would know the name I was going by. If he'd been watching me for any time at all it wouldn't have taken long to discover my alias. I leaned forward and said softly, "Everyone here knows me as Kate. I'd appreciate it if you'd call me that too."

"Well look at that. I want something from you and you want something from me. Maybe we can trade."

"What do you mean?" I asked, suspicious.

"I don't think it's asking too much to let me feel our baby move. Do you?"

"Well, since our baby is inside of my body, that would involve you touching me, which I'm not okay with just now."

"Okay. Well you just let me know when you're ready, Lily and that's when I'll start calling you Kate."

So far this meeting was not going very well. I felt off-balance. I needed to gain control. "How's Amanda doing?"

"How should I know?"

"I thought she was your girlfriend."

"Like I keep telling you, she's just a friend."

"It didn't look like that way when I saw you kissing her."

His eyebrows drew together. "And when did this supposedly happen?"

"The day I came to Reno and took back my stuff."

AT first he didn't respond, probably trying to come up with an excuse. "Why should I believe you?"

"I know what I saw. You're not the only who knows how to spy on someone," I said, starting to feel in control.

"Well, Lily," he said, exaggerating my name. "I don't remember kissing her."

"Just so you know, Trevor," I said, exaggerating his name. "If someone hears you call me Lily, all bets are off and I'll have no reason to let you feel the baby move."

He sat back against the booth, frowning. "Fine. You win that one. But I hope you'll consider it, at least." His voice softened as he said, "That is my child too, you know."

My heart softened a bit at not only his words but his tone of voice. "We'll see." I didn't want to commit to anything yet.

The waitress arrived and set our food in front of us. I nibbled at my sandwich while Trevor dug into his burger.

"Do you have the divorce papers?" I asked.

Trevor set his food down and swallowed the bite he'd been chewing. "They're back in my hotel room."

"What needs to be done for it to be final?"

"I just need your signature, then it will be done."

His gaze locked on mine and I found that the incredible blue of his eyes still had the power to draw me in.

"Lily." He shook his head. "Sorry, I mean Kate. It's not too late, you know. We don't have to go through with this. We can still be a family. You, me, and our baby."

He reached across the table and took my hand. Though I wanted to pull my hand away, I found I was hungry for the touch of another person. His hand was warm and strong and for a moment the love I'd had for him washed over me.

"Please. Give me one more chance," he said.

His eyes matched the tone of his voice and I found myself believing that he really did want to be with me. Gently, I pulled my hand away and rested it in my lap, but the feeling of tenderness lingered.

Though my heart was warming to Trevor, my head knew I needed to be wary. I called up some of the less pleasant times in our marriage to remind myself why I had left. The feelings that came with those memories crowded out the tenderness that had been growing.

"Trevor, you have to understand. The way you treated me killed my love for you, little by little."

"Are you saying you don't care about me at all?"

The hurt in his eyes was clear and I found that even though my love for him was damaged, it had not been destroyed.

"I do care about you," I said. "But it's not the same as it was before."

"What do you mean?"

I rubbed my forehead, wondering how much I should say. I didn't want to open myself up entirely—that would just give him the ammunition he needed to hurt me. "In the beginning I loved you completely. You hadn't done anything to hurt me yet. And the time leading up to our wedding and right after were wonderful. But soon after the wedding you let your jealousy get in the way of our relationship. Justin and I were never anything but friends, but you couldn't see that and you imagined that more was going on."

I noticed that at the mention of Justin's name, Trevor's jaw clenched. Obviously he still had issues there.

"You wouldn't believe me," I continued, "when I told you it was only you that I loved. Your lack of trust in me ended up pushing me away. But Trevor, the worst was when you hurt me. Physically and emotionally. I can never be with you as long as I think you might hurt me."

He seemed to be making an effort to get himself under control. "Now you're not believing me when I tell you I've changed. How can you accuse me of not believing you, but then you refuse to believe me?"

I bit my lip, wondering how honest I could be with him now. If I brought up all of his past mistakes, how would he react? Was it even fair for me to throw them all back at him? But we needed to discuss them. It wasn't like I was trying to hurt him. We just needed to clear the air. Even if we never got back together, we would still have a child to raise together. We needed to be able to talk about our past.

"Trevor, why should I believe you now? Have you forgotten all the lies you told me and how you lied to your parents about me?"

"When did I ever lie to you?"

This is where I needed to be careful. I didn't know if he realized I was the one who had called in a tip to the police saying it might be Rob's Auto Body shop that was involved in the car thefts. If he didn't suspect me, and I didn't know why he would, I certainly didn't want to give myself away. He probably didn't even know that I knew why he had been in jail. "For one thing," I said, "You told me you weren't drinking but you still were. And when I was sick in the beginning of my pregnancy, not only did you lock me into our apartment and take my purse with my keys and wallet, but you took all of the money in my bank account."

He rubbed his hand on his chin. "Look, I know I made a lot of mistakes. But in the six months since you've been gone I've come to realize what's most important, and that's you. I don't know what else to tell you to convince you."

"I need time to think about this," I said. "A few hours ago I didn't even know you were in town."

His hand slid across the table, but I left mine in my lap. He rested his hand on the table as he spoke. "I'm sorry if I scared you when I showed up. I'm sorry for all the things I did that made you want to leave me. But I still love you with all my heart and I want to make our marriage work." He paused. "Just think about it. I'll be here again tomorrow at one o'clock. I hope you'll come talk to me."

"Thanks for lunch, Trevor." I slid out of the booth and stood. "I'll think about it, but no promises."

He smiled and nodded and I walked out the door and to my car, my mind in turmoil.

CHAPTER THIRTY-FOUR

I drove home in a daze. Fortunately, I'd driven the route often enough that I didn't have to think about where I was going. A short time later I pulled into my gravel drive and parked in front of my house. Greta was happy to see me and I scratched her in her favorite spots for a few minutes as I sat on the couch.

Today was one of the days I didn't have classes. I usually used the time to do homework, but there would be no way I would be able to concentrate. As I replayed my conversation with Trevor, multiple feelings went through me. At first I had been terrified when he'd walked through the door of *Billi's*, but he had actually been quite reasonable. At lunch I had even felt some renewed tenderness for him. And when he had taken my hand in his, I had been hungry for his touch.

My biggest concern was whether he meant what he said or if he had some other agenda. Did he suspect that I had taken his money? Or did he truly love me and want to be with me? But most important, had he changed, as he claimed? I desperately wanted to believe him. Things would be so much easier if my life could get back on track and if the family I had always visualized for myself could actually come to fruition.

But I had doubts. Serious doubts. And I didn't know how I could test Trevor to see if he was telling the truth. The only way I could think of was to give him a chance. He'd already found me, so there was no risk in spending time with him. As long as I kept my guard up, I felt I would be okay.

The next day at work, toward the end of my shift, I kept glancing out the window toward the diner to try to catch a glimpse of Trevor arriving. I hadn't decided yet if I was going to go talk to him—I was still scared because I was unsure of his motives.

At twelve thirty I saw his blue Camaro pull up to the diner and I felt my heart race. I watched as he opened the door of his car and stepped out. He looked in my direction, although I was fairly certain he couldn't see me through the glass, then walked into the diner.

I found myself feeling like I did when I lived in Reno and Trevor was just starting to notice me. I craved his attention and approval. I *needed* him to notice me and want me. Even though he had treated me poorly, my loneliness over the previous six months made me want to overlook the mistakes of the past.

But I did need to find out about his arrest. Was he involved with the car thefts? Where did he get the two-hundred thousand dollars? I knew I couldn't be with someone who was stealing.

Maddy showed up a little while later and I left the store, then stood on the sidewalk in front, unsure what I should do. Then I started walking toward my car, too scared to do anything else.

"Lily!"

I froze as Trevor's voice rang out. Then I continued walking.

"Kate!"

This time I stopped and turned in his direction. He was jogging across the street toward me.

"Sorry. I forgot about the name thing," he said, smiling.

I tentatively smiled back.

"I saw you standing on the sidewalk and I was afraid you weren't going to come talk to me." He paused. "And then you started walking away."

Suddenly I felt bad about my decision. For a moment I put myself in Trevor's place. His wife had left him and he had spent months looking for her, and now that he'd found her, she didn't seem to want to have anything to do with him. My heart sank as I imagined how I would feel.

But I had to keep reminding myself why I'd left and what had led up to it. He had made choices that had pushed me away. These were just the consequences of those choices.

Thinking in those terms made me feel better.

"Will you talk to me today, Kate?" He shook his head. "I don't know if I'll ever get used to calling you that."

"I have classes this afternoon, Trevor. I don't really have time right now."

"Oh." He paused, considering. "When will you have time?"

"Tomorrow afternoon, I guess."

"Okay. I'll be waiting."

"Fine." I stood there a moment. "I have to get going."

His blue eyes bored into mine and he whispered, "I love you, Lily."

A lump formed in my throat as I looked into his eyes and his words penetrated my heart. "Bye, Trevor," I managed to say, then I turned and walked to my car. I didn't look in his direction until I was safely in my car. He was still standing where I'd left him, watching me, a look of despair on his face.

I backed out of the parking spot and began the drive to class as tears filled my eyes and rolled down my cheeks.

I had a hard time focusing in my classes. Finals were in just a few weeks and I looked forward to getting those done. And then my baby would be coming. The closer my due date came, the more excited I became. The baby's room was ready—all it needed was a baby.

Finally it was time to go home. I fixed myself dinner, then played with Greta for a while. It was too cold to play outside, so I used a toy rope and played tug-of-war with her. She had gotten a lot bigger since I'd gotten her and just having her around made me feel more secure.

All of a sudden she dropped her end of the rope and ran to the front door, barking. It was dark outside, but as I looked out the front window I could see a car pulling up the gravel drive. As the car got closer, I saw it was Trevor's Camaro.

Panic engulfed me. What was he doing here? Why had he come? Should I hide in the secret room? What would he do if I didn't answer the door? What would he do when he heard Greta barking?

CHAPTER THIRTY-FIVE

I ran upstairs and into the baby's room, then looked out the window. Trevor was getting out of his car. It was dark out, but I could see him hesitate before walking toward the front porch. I lost sight of him but heard knocking. Greta was still barking like crazy with her deep, loud voice.

Since my car was parked out front, Trevor would know I was home. Slowly, I walked out of the baby's room, then down the stairs. As I approached the front door, Trevor knocked again. I peered through the peephole and saw Trevor patiently waiting. I turned the lock and reached for the door knob, then hesitated.

"Lily?" Trevor called, obviously hearing me turn the deadbolt.

With me there, Greta had calmed down and only let out an occasional bark. Slowly, I turned the knob, then pulled open the door. "What are you doing here, Trevor?" My voice was less than friendly and I held Greta's collar to keep her from running out.

The smile he'd had on his face vanished. "I didn't want to wait until tomorrow to talk to you, so I thought I'd stop by." He took a step back. "I'm sorry. I didn't think it would be a big deal." Trevor glanced at Greta. "Look, if you don't want me here, I'll leave."

I sighed. "You're already here, so you might as well come in."

His smile returned.

I opened the door and allowed him to enter. Once the door was closed I let go of Greta. She had gotten better about not jumping on people, but she still went to Trevor, who was standing just inside the front door, and vigorously sniffed him.

Trevor laughed, then squatted down and let Greta smell his hand. After Greta had her fill, she licked his hand and he pet her.

I wondered if I'd ruined any chance of her protecting me from Trevor now that she'd met him, but then I remembered the time Marcus had been teaching me self-defense and Greta had gotten upset and growled at him. And she had been familiar with him.

"I didn't know you liked dogs, Lily." He stood back up. "Is it okay if I call you Lily while we're alone?"

"I guess it's okay while we're here. But yeah, I've never had a dog before. I got Greta so I would have a guard dog. She does a pretty good job too."

"When I heard her barking I was a little worried you'd send her after me."

I laughed, thinking how I'd gotten her specifically because of Trevor. "Do you want to sit down?"

"Sure." He followed me to the couch.

When he sat on one end, I sat as far from his as I could.

"How's school?" he asked.

"Good. I have finals in just a few weeks." I thought back to the last time I was getting ready for finals. It was the previous semester, right after I'd found out I was pregnant. When Trevor had brought me back from the motel I'd run to, he wouldn't let me leave and I'd missed finals, failing all of my classes. Anger welled up in me as I thought about what he'd done.

"I think it's awesome that you're still going to school." He stared at the floor for a minute, then looked at me. "I'm really sorry about what I did. How I didn't let you finish the semester. That was really stupid and selfish of me."

Though I appreciated his apology, it didn't change what had happened. "I'm still pretty mad about that, Trevor. The whole semester was wasted. Not to mention all the money I spent. Why did you do that?"

"I just didn't want you to leave. I was sure that if you walked out the door without me, you'd never come back."

My eyebrows went up. "How did that work out for you?"

He laughed uncomfortably. "Not so good."

We were both quiet for a minute, then I asked, "Why did you want that gym bag back so bad?"

The question obviously caught him off-guard. "Well, it's not that I wanted it back so bad. I was, uh, I was just mad at you for wanting the divorce. And I, uh, it was the only thing I could think of to demand from you."

I could tell he knew that was a lame excuse. "Since I sent it back, I expect you to keep your promise. We need to get this divorce finalized."

"I know, I know. I just wanted to spend some time with you. I hoped you might change your mind."

I didn't want to get on that subject again so I asked him another question that had been on my mind. "You never told me why you were in jail. What was that all about?"

"Apparently the police thought Rob and I were involved in stealing cars. But they didn't have enough evidence, so they had to let us go."

"You say that like they were right about you, but just couldn't prove it."

"No, they were wrong. We didn't steal any cars."

Somehow I couldn't quite believe him and I just wasn't in the mood to try. "Look, Trevor. I'm really tired and it's getting late. Maybe we can do this another time."

"Lily, will you let me feel the baby moving?" He moved to the edge of the couch, like he was about to get up.

"She's sleeping right now."

"She? Do you think it's a girl?"

"Yeah. I think it might be," I said smoothly. "But there's no point in trying to feel her moving, because she's not moving right now."

"Is that normal?" he asked, looking alarmed.

I laughed. "Yes. She has to sleep sometime. She doesn't move constantly."

"Oh. As you can tell, I don't know anything about pregnancy." He seemed to hesitate. "And since I haven't been involved so far, I don't feel part of it at all."

Guilt sliced through me. He *had* been left completely out of the experience. But that was his own fault, I reminded myself. I had always wanted to share this with him, but his actions had forced me to leave. Then I felt the baby move. Maybe I should get this over with, I thought. "Trevor, I think she just woke up, if you want to feel."

Eagerly he moved to sit next to me. Our legs touched and I felt a jolt.

"Where should I put my hands?" He held his hands over my belly.

Flustered to have him so close to me, at first I didn't answer.

"Lily?" he asked.

"Right," I said and glanced at him. Then I reached for his hands, but hesitated to touch them.

"Lily?" he asked, his voice soft.

My gaze met his and I was drawn in by his vivid blue eyes. Pulling my gaze away, I set my hands in my lap. "You can just put your hands on my stomach."

"Like this?" he asked, setting his hands on my large belly.

I could feel the baby moving, but not where he'd put his hands. There wasn't a good way to describe where he needed to move them, so I forced myself to put my hands on top of his and slide them to the right spot. Ignoring his gaze, I held his hands where the baby was most active.

"Whoa! I felt it kick!"

Despite everything, I couldn't help smiling. I knew the excitement of feeling the baby move for the first time.

"That's so cool!" he said. "It moved again!"

I rolled my eyes. "You can say 'she'."

"But what if it's a boy?"

I lifted my hands from his. "It's a girl, Trevor."

"But you don't know for sure. It could be a boy."

"Trevor. I had an ultrasound and I found out it's a girl. For sure."

"Oh." He took his hands off my stomach. "Why did you tell me you didn't know then?"

"I guess I was just so surprised to see you, and I was kind of mad too. So I didn't want to tell you."

"Okay. What do you think we should name her?"

I already had a name in mind and I had never considered that Trevor would want any input. I hadn't visualized him in this process at all. "I don't know. Do you have any names that you like?"

"Well, I hadn't actually thought about it. I guess I need to get one of those baby name books."

"I have one you can look at if you want." I went in to the kitchen and grabbed the baby name book off of the counter. I had been looking at it earlier. When I came back to the couch I sat next to Trevor. It's not that I wanted to sit close to him exactly, but since we were going to look at the book, it just made sense to sit next to each other.

I handed him the book and he turned to the girl names section. He pointed out a few names, but I had already settled on one that I liked. Natalie. As we worked our way to the N's, I waited to see if he would notice the name I wanted. He skipped right over it.

"What about Natalie?" I asked.

"Natalie, huh? Yeah, it's okay." He looked at me. "Is that the name you want to give her?"

"I like it."

"Then Natalie is fine with me."

Warmth flowed over me at his willingness to accept my choice.

"Really?"

"Of course. You're the mother. I think you should choose."

I smiled, feeling better about Trevor than I had in a while. "She's kicking again. Do you want to feel?"

He nodded and I guided his hands to the right spot, then watched as his face lit up.

"What does it feel like when the movement is inside of you?" he asked.

"It's kind of hard to explain. But it's different than from the outside, that's for sure." I paused, considering my next words. "Sometimes I can see her move right under my skin."

"What do you mean?"

"When I look at my belly, under my shirt, sometimes I can see my skin ripple as she rolls around in there."

"Can you show me?" he asked, his face hopeful.

Before I had said anything, I knew if I told him he'd want to see. Now I wondered if I should have kept it to myself. He obviously saw my hesitation.

"Please, Lily?"

"Okay. I guess it would be all right." Slowly, I lifted my blouse and exposed my swollen belly. We both stared at it, waiting. Suddenly there was a large ripple as Natalie moved in my womb.

Trevor laughed. "That's so weird, but cool at the same time."

I laughed too. "I know. It's strange to think there's a miniature human being inside of me."

"Can I feel it?"

I nodded.

He placed his hands against my skin and I almost gasped with the heat that raced through me. In my peripheral vision I saw him glance at me and I wondered if he could tell the effect he had on me.

Then, slowly, his hands moved around on my stomach. I didn't know if he was trying to find where the baby was moving, or if he had something else in mind. In either case, I had to admit to myself that I liked his touch. I'd had so little human touch in the last six months that it was almost like I was starving for the warm touch that he was providing.

My mind wandered back to the first month of our marriage, before things had turned sour. The feelings he elicited from me now were similar to that time. I leaned my head against the couch cushions and closed my eyes. His hands continued to gently stroke my stomach. It felt so good that I didn't want him to stop.

Even though my eyes were closed, I could tell he was moving closer to me. Suddenly I felt his lips pressing against mine.

"Lily," he murmured. "I've missed you so much."

I opened my eyes and saw his face very close to mine. The blue of his eyes pulled me in and, right then, I wanted to be in his embrace. My arms went around his neck and he kissed me again, but this time his tongue pushed its way into my mouth and I eagerly responded.

After a moment, he stood and held out his hand. I took it and he helped me up, then he led me upstairs to my bedroom.

CHAPTER THIRTY-SIX

In the middle of the night I woke and was startled to find Trevor sleeping beside me. It only took a moment to recall the previous night. Being intimate with him made me feel emotionally close to him, but I wasn't sure if I should have done it. Now it would be harder to push the divorce through. And I suspected he would be more resistant.

Though I had enjoyed our time together, the underlying problems hadn't changed. He had been abusive, locked me up, stolen from me, and been arrested on suspicion of car theft. Not to mention the fact that he had buried two-hundred thousand dollars that came from some unknown and probably illegal source. Money that I now had and needed to give back. I didn't want to have anything to do with it.

I hadn't figured out how to get it back to him without divulging the fact that I had dug it up and taken it home. I wondered what his true motives were in coming here. He hadn't acted like he thought I had found the SD card and knew anything about the money. Could it be that he really did love me? What about the kiss I'd seen him share with Amanda?

One thing I knew for sure: I couldn't trust him.

I didn't want him in the house when it was time for me to go to work. Though I didn't think he'd come across the hidden room, I didn't want to take a chance. I sat up and looked at him for a minute.

"Trevor," I said, shaking him. "Trevor, wake up."

"What? What time is it?" he asked, groggy.

"It's one thirty in the morning."

"Go back to sleep."

"Trevor," I said louder as I shook him with more force. "It's time for you to leave. I don't want you to spend the night."

"Why not?" He sat up too, more awake now.

"I just don't." I didn't feel like I had to give an explanation. This was my home and if I wanted him to leave, he would just have to leave.

"Don't be ridiculous, Lily. It's the middle of the night. Why can't I wait until morning to leave?"

There was no question that he was irritated by my request. "I have to get up early for work, and I don't want you here when I'm gone."

He lay back down. "I can leave when you do."

Now I was irritated. He was completely ignoring my demand.

He put his arm around me. "Come on, Lily. Let's go back to sleep."

Feeling helpless, I lay down and felt his hands start to caress me. I wasn't in the mood for what he so clearly wanted, especially after his refusal to listen to my wants. I pushed his hand away, but he put it back, again ignoring my message.

"No, Trevor," I said as I sat up.

"What do you mean,'No'?"

"What do you think I mean? I don't want to do that with you."

He laughed. "Why not? You were completely willing last night."

"Well, now I'm not willing."

He sat up next to me. "I don't get you, Lily."

"What do you mean?"

"First you run away, then I find you and you're all standoffish. Then I come over and you seem to want me as much as I want you. Now you're all cold again."

Was I being unreasonable? I shook my head, knowing I wasn't. I had just made a mistake last night. The loneliness had gotten the better of me and I had given in. But how could I convince Trevor of that? Now he seemed to think that everything was back to normal.

"I really think you need to go."

"And what if I don't want to go," he said, annoyance clear on his face.

"I guess I could always call the police." I didn't know if I would really do that, but I hoped the threat would be enough to make him leave.

He reached across me, startling me, and grabbed my cell phone from the bedside table. "I don't think so," he said.

"Trevor, what are you doing?"

"I'm taking your phone so you can't call the police. This is between us."

"Give me back my phone," I said, alarmed by his behavior.

"Lily, I love you." His voice was soft. "Why can't you accept that? I'm your husband. You're my wife. We're having a baby and we need to be a family."

It seemed his controlling ways had not stopped. I don't know why I had thought he might have changed. I guess I was so lonesome that I was willing to believe what I wanted to believe. "Trevor," I started, worried how he would react. "I don't think this was a good idea."

"You don't think what was a good idea?"

"You coming to my house. Me letting you in. Us ending up here." I spread my hands out, encompassing my bedroom.

"Why not?"

"I'm sorry, but I don't think it's going to work out between us."

"Again, why not?"

His anger was ratcheting up and I was beginning to feel scared as well as nervous about where this conversation would end. "I don't think you've changed as much as you think you have." I tried to speak in a non-confrontational manner, hoping it would defuse any anger he was feeling.

"Oh come on, Lily. You've hardly given me a chance. We've spent, what, less than a day together? And that's all it took for you to come to your conclusion? I don't think you're even trying." He stared at me as he chewed on his lower lip. "There's someone else, isn't there?"

"No. There isn't," I said with vehemence. "I swear."

"I find that hard to believe," he said, throwing back the covers.

I hoped that meant he was going to leave. But I felt like he was making my point for me and I had to point it out. "See, Trevor? The way you're accusing me shows me you haven't changed. You're jumping to the same old conclusions."

He grabbed his jeans from the floor and yanked them on. "Why should I believe you? You've lied to me before."

"What? When?"

He sneered at me. "Just tonight you admitted you lied to me about knowing we were having a girl. And then when you came to Reno and said you wanted to meet me at Circus Circus, but you were really luring me away so you could get your stuff." He glared at me. "What else have you lied to me about, Lily?"

Wow. And he doesn't even know about the two-hundred thousand I have stashed in the next room. He would go ballistic if he knew about that.

Is he right though? Have I been lying to him as much as he has lied to me? No, I don't think so. The circumstances were different. I lied to him about meeting him for my own protection. But I probably shouldn't have lied about knowing the baby is a girl. But when he's lied to me, it's been to purposefully deceive me. How can I believe him now when he says he loves me?

"I'm sorry I lied to you about the baby, Trevor. And the thing in Reno was just because I was scared." I hesitated. "But Trevor, I think you're still lying to me. I saw you kiss Amanda that day. I was waiting for you to leave and I was watching and I saw you kiss her."

He shook his head. "You're wrong. I've never kissed her. Why would I when it's you that I want?"

I knew what I had seen. There was no mistake. He had kissed her.

Why was he pretending otherwise? What else had he lied to me about that I didn't even know about?"

"Whatever," I finally said, not interested in arguing about it. "Can I have my phone back?" I held out my hand.

"Here."

He tossed it onto the bed and I grabbed it before he could take it back.

"Thank you." I watched as he finished getting dressed. When he was done, he sat on the edge of the bed and gazed at me.

"I don't know what else to do to convince you of how I feel," he said. "I love you and I don't want this divorce."

Oh, Trevor, I wanted to say. I wish we could make it work too. But I can't live with a controlling, jealous, angry husband and I don't believe you're willing to change.

I closed my eyes and imperceptibly shook my head. When I opened my eyes and my gaze met his, his expression wavered between sadness and fury.

"Just so you know, Lily, I'm planning on being part of my daughter's life." He paused as an idea seemed to occur to him. He smiled suddenly, but he didn't seem happy. Instead, the smile had a tinge of vindictiveness. "You know what I'm going to do? I'm going to move to this little town so that I can see my baby whenever I want. What do you think about that?"

No! I silently screamed as my head began to pound. I don't want you here!

"And don't even think about running off again. Because no matter where you go, I'll find you. I have every right to be in my baby girl's life and I plan on doing all within my power to make sure she knows her daddy."

Feeling shaky, I tried to control my voice. "I think that's great, Trevor," I lied. "You should move here. That will make it easier with the baby." I paused. "Do you think you'll be able to find a job?"

I could tell my statement had surprised him. "Yeah, sure," he said. "I'll be able to find a job. Don't worry about me."

"By the way, when are you going to bring over the divorce papers for me to sign?"

"I don't know why you're in such a big hurry."

"I just want to get it over with," I said with a frown.

"I'll get to it eventually. But right now, I'm out of here."

Relieved he was finally leaving, I followed him to the front door. He opened the door, then stopped and turned to me, a smirk on his face. "Thanks for having me over."

"Bye, Trevor," I said, regretting answering the door earlier that evening.

He walked out and I locked the door behind him. Though it was still dark outside, when I looked through the peephole I was able to see him get into his car. A moment later he turned his car around and drove down the gravel drive. I watched until he was gone.

I went back up to bed, but couldn't fall asleep, thinking about the ramifications of him moving here.

CHAPTER THIRTY-SEVEN

The next day at work I kept looking out the window to see if Trevor was in the area. Once I saw a man who I thought could be Trevor, but I had only caught a glimpse and couldn't be sure. All day long I was distracted and stressed and Billi noticed.

"Is something wrong, Kate?" she asked, catching me looking out the window yet again.

I spun around, embarrassed. "No. I just thought I saw someone I knew."

"Okay. By the way, I hired two new girls to help out at Christmas. Hopefully one of them will work out to replace you when the baby comes."

"Oh. That's great." Though I knew I didn't want to work once the baby came, I also knew I'd miss my job. I'd enjoyed interacting with the customers and everyone had always been friendly. But I'd told Billi I was going to quit once the baby came, so of course she'd hired a replacement for me. It just felt strange to be told I was being replaced.

When my shift was over I stayed alert as I walked to my car, expecting Trevor to appear out of nowhere. I didn't have classes that afternoon, so I drove straight home, keeping an eye on the cars around me, looking for Trevor's blue Camaro. I didn't see it and once in my house, I locked the front door.

All afternoon I felt nervous, not knowing if Trevor would unexpectedly show up.

I can't live like this, I thought. But what can I do? Trevor isn't doing anything illegal. At least not yet. I just need to relax and try to live my life.

Once evening came, I fixed dinner then cleaned up. Once I felt everything was clean enough to allow me to unwind, I took my eReader into the living room and curled up on the couch. It was about seven o'clock and dark out. As I settled into the book, I finally felt myself relaxing. Greta was curled up in the corner on her pet bed, her head resting on her paws.

Suddenly, she jumped up and ran to the door, her tail wagging. Then she began barking. My heart pounded. Obviously, someone was coming. Then there was a loud knock at the door. Startled, I let out a little scream and felt the blood drain from my face.

I went to the window and lifted a slat on the blinds, peering out. From the light coming from the porch, I was able to see enough to know that Trevor's car was not out front. Who could it be? Was Trevor trying to scare me? If he was, it was working.

Quietly, I tiptoed to the door and looked out the peephole. When I saw Marcus there, I almost wept with relief. I took several deep breaths, trying to get myself under control, then opened the door.

"Marcus, what a nice surprise. I haven't seen you in a long time."

"Hi, Kate," he said, a broad smile on his face, his incredible green eyes sparkling. "How have you been?" He glanced at my stomach. "You've really . . . grown." He laughed.

"I know. I feel huge. Do you want to come in?"

"Sure."

He followed me to the couch and we both sat down. I hadn't seen him since the night he'd told me he had gotten back together with Marissa, about four months earlier. "How are you? How's Marissa?"

At the mention of her name, his smile dimmed. "We broke up."

"Oh. I'm sorry."

"No, it's okay. It was my decision."

"Oh. Well, how's your job going?"

"It's fantastic. How about you? How's school going?"

"Great. It's almost time for finals. But you already knew that. You're going to school too, right?"

"Yes. It's funny though. When I was in high school I just did what I had to to get by. But somehow it's different now. I'm really enjoying learning. I'm glad I went back."

"I know what you mean."

"So do you have the baby's room ready?"

"Yes. Your dad helped me get the dresser and changing table set up. And when I found out it was going to be a girl, I added some feminine touches to the room.

"A girl, huh? That's great. Have you thought of a name yet?"

"Yes. Natalie."

"I like it."

I smiled, pleased that he approved. "Do you want to see her room?"

"Sure. I haven't been in it for a long time."

"Okay. Let's go."

We walked up the stairs and into Natalie's room.

Marcus looked around. "It turned out great, Kate. You're a natural decorator."

I laughed. "I don't know about that, but thanks."

Then I heard pounding on the front door. I walked to the window and looked out. Even in the dark I was able to see it was Trevor's blue Camaro.

"Are you expecting someone?" Marcus asked.

"No." I hoped if I didn't answer the door, Trevor would leave.

That hope was quickly dashed as I heard the front door open and Trevor walk in, calling for me. "Lily? Lily, where are you?"

I glanced at Marcus, who looked completely confused.

"Stay here," I said, then I hurried out of the room and down the stairs.

"There you are, Lily," Trevor said loudly.

The smell hit me first. "You've been drinking." I tried to talk normally so as not to rouse Trevor's suspicion, yet quiet enough so Marcus wouldn't hear.

"What was your first clue?"

"What are you doing here? I told you not to come here anymore."

"I wanted to come see my wife, of course. Why else would I come here?"

"Please, Trevor. Keep your voice down."

His eyes narrowed. "Why?"

Thinking fast, I said, "The baby finally stopped kicking and I don't want you to wake her up."

"Oh."

"You need to leave now."

"Why would I do that? I want to spend the evening with my beautiful wife."

"Just go. Please."

Then I heard a creaking noise coming from the stairs.

Turning, I saw Marcus at the bottom of the stairs.

"Who the hell are you?" Trevor shouted, suddenly livid.

"Is everything okay, Kate?"

Panic flowed over me in waves, threatening to drown me. "Everything's fine," I managed to say.

"Who are you?" Marcus asked Trevor, clearly concerned for me.

"I'm her husband."

Marcus' eyes widened in shock and his eyes shifted to me. "Kate?"

Trevor started laughing hysterically and Marcus and I both turned to him.

"I see she's got you fooled," Trevor said, trying to catch his breath between laughs.

"Trevor, leave. Now!" I demanded.

He ignored me as he focused on Marcus. "What else did she tell you?"

"Kate?" Marcus asked again.

"Her name's Lily, you idiot," Trevor said, his laughter under control.

Marcus just stared, first at Trevor, then at me. More than anything in the world, I wanted to disappear, just sink into the floor and never come up.

"I'd better get going, Kate, uh . . . yeah," Marcus said as he walked toward the door.

"Marcus, wait. I can explain," I said.

"You don't have to explain anything to me. I'll see you around."

With that, he walked out, shutting the door behind him.

I was so angry at Trevor, I thought I would explode.

"Are you sleeping with him too?" he asked.

My hand swung up and across his face before I'd completed thinking about doing it. He staggered back, caught off-guard. Then I moved backwards, out of his reach, expecting him to retaliate.

"Why was he upstairs? Was I interrupting something, Kate?" He exaggerated my alias as he rubbed his face.

"He's just a friend," I said with as much venom as I could muster.

"Yeah, right. I know how that works."

I closed my eyes and shook my head, knowing there wasn't a way to make him realize he was wrong, and knowing he hadn't changed at all. Not even a little bit.

"Get out of my house before I call the police." This time I had my cell phone in my pocket, but I didn't reach for it, not wanting Trevor to know it was there.

He took a step toward me, his body language conveying his intention to hurt me, but stopped short when Greta growled at him.

Relief cascaded over me and my love for my sweet Greta grew immensely.

He looked at her and she bared her teeth and barked menacingly.

"I don't need this," Trevor muttered before turning away from me and walking out the door.

As soon as I'd locked the door, I burst into tears and sank to the floor. Greta pressed up against me and I wrapped my arms around her. "You're such a good dog," I sobbed. "Such a good girl." She licked my face until I couldn't help but laugh.

Once I'd gotten my emotions under control, I looked out the blinds to make sure Trevor had left, then checked the back door to make sure it was locked. I turned on the TV and stared at the program that was on, not really watching.

I tried to grasp what had happened and what the consequences would be. Trevor knew that Marcus was in my life. He assumed he was my boyfriend and now he would be less cooperative about the divorce than before. Marcus had broken up with Marissa and had come to see me, but now he probably thought I was a liar, which I guess I was, and a married woman, which I guess I was too.

What a mess I'd made. I'd come here to make a fresh start, but now in some ways, things were worse than ever.

When I was too exhausted to think, I trudged up to bed, but slept fitfully all night, terrified that Trevor would come back and hurt me and the baby. Thankfully I had Greta with me. I knew she would protect me.

CHAPTER THIRTY-EIGHT

The next day I didn't have to work. The first thing I did was call an alarm company and have an alarm system put in. After jotting down the security code and putting it under the silverware holder in the kitchen drawer, I wondered how much safer the burglar alarm really made me. If the alarm was tripped, it would take the police a little time to reach me, but I didn't know what else to do. I was set to deliver my baby in just a matter of weeks. I had a doctor I'd been seeing and I didn't think running was the right answer. I just had to do all within my power to stay safe. I had Greta and now I had the alarm.

Over the next three weeks I didn't see Trevor or Marcus. I wasn't surprised not to see Marcus, but I was nervous that Trevor hadn't made an appearance. I was constantly on edge, expecting him to show up when I was least prepared.

I was able to get through finals, which was a relief, then I settled in to wait to have my baby. A few days before my due date, it was my last day of work. I was afraid I'd be bored at home, just waiting, but I was so big now that it was uncomfortable to work anyway.

Though my baby was due any day, I decided to put up some Christmas decorations. Christmas was two weeks away and after I'd gone to all the trouble of getting my ornaments back, the least I could do was put them up. I drove to a nearby Christmas tree lot and bought a small tree, one that I could manage on my own.

Setting it up in the living room, I arranged my favorite ornaments on the tree and stood back, having a nice reminder of my childhood home. Warmth flowed through me as I thought back to the Christmases I'd spent with my dad. He'd always made an extra effort to make me feel special. Though I didn't have any presents under the tree, I enjoyed the way the tree made the room feel more festive. Anyway, I didn't need any presents—my new baby was the only present I wanted.

When my due date came and went, I felt disappointed and started to believe the baby would never come. Finally, two days later, my water broke. I wasn't having any contractions yet, but knew I should get to the hospital. Scared to drive myself, I gathered the courage to call Trish and ask her to drive me to the hospital.

"Of course I'll take you. I'll be right there," she said.

A few minutes later she pulled up to the house. I hurried out, my overnight bag in my hand, and made sure to set the alarm before locking the door.

"How are you feeling?" Trish asked as I climbed into her car.

"Okay. I haven't had any contractions yet." I paused. "I'm worried about my dog, Greta, though. I don't have anyone to feed her while I'm gone."

"I'd be happy to do it for you, Kate."

I noticed she glanced at me when she said my name. Fairly certain Marcus had told her what had happened with Trevor several weeks before, I was mortified at what she must think of me and I ignored the implied question.

"I would really appreciate it." I pulled my keys out of my purse and set them in the cup holder. Then I told her the alarm code. "Please make sure to set it when you leave."

"Okay."

A short time later we pulled up to the hospital

"Do you want me to come in with you?" she asked.

As the reality of what was happening became clear, I began to feel scared. I had some idea of what to expect, but since I had never been through giving birth before there was still so much I didn't know. I longed to have someone with me to comfort me and support me. "Yes, I'd like that."

We pulled into a parking space and walked in to the hospital together. I had pre-registered so it didn't take long before we were taken to the labor and delivery area.

Trish waited in the hall while I got settled into a room. Hailey, the nurse assigned to me, checked my progress. It was still very early, but since my water had broken, they would keep me there.

Hailey put a monitor around my belly and Natalie's heartbeat filled the room, loud and strong. A few minutes later Trish came in and sat by the bed.

"Are you sure you want me here, Kate?"

"If you don't mind, I'd like you to stay." Tears filled my eyes as I thought how pathetic I was. I barely knew my neighbor but I had no one else to be with me.

"I don't mind," she assured me with a warm smile.

A short time later I began having contractions. They were bearable, but I rested my head on the pillow and closed my eyes. After two hours, labor was not progressing very fast, so my doctor ordered Pitocin to get things going.

Soon after they gave me the Pitocin the labor pains became stronger. The nurse helped me with my breathing and I was better able to deal with the increased pain. Trish left for a while to get something to eat and when she came back she wasn't alone.

"Marcus!" I said, delighted to see him. Even though I didn't look my best, I was thrilled to see a friendly face.

He walked into the room as Trish stepped out. "I wasn't sure if I should come," he said, obviously uncertain if I wanted him there.

"I'm so glad you came," I said. Then a powerful contraction overwhelmed me. Closing my eyes, I focused on my breathing. When I opened my eyes, I smiled at the look of terror on Marcus' face.

"Should I get the nurse?" he asked.

"No, it's okay. Come sit by me." I motioned to the empty chair next to the bed and he sat down.

"Does it hurt a lot?" he asked.

"Yes. It does. But I just need to focus on what the end result will be."

He laughed nervously. "Yeah, I guess."

"I'm so glad you came, Marcus. Your mom has been so nice to stay, but I'm sure she has other things to do." I hesitated, wondering if I was assuming too much. "Can you stay for a while?"

He grinned. "I'll stay as long as you want me to."

"Really? Thank you." Another contraction hit me and I focused on dealing with that. When it was over I looked at Marcus. "I want to explain about what happened that night." I was certain he knew what night I was talking about.

"You can explain it to me later. Right now you need to focus on you and your baby. Okay?"

"Okay," I said as another, even stronger contraction rolled over me. As it faded I felt tears start. "Oh, Marcus, it hurts so much. I don't know if I can do this."

He took my hand. "It's okay, Kate. I'll stay right next to you. You're doing great."

"Another one's starting," I managed to say before a powerful wave of pain nearly crushed me. "I can't stand it," I gasped as it began to subside.

"Do you want me to get the nurse?" he asked, looking panicked.

"Yes," I whispered.

He raced from the room and a moment later Hailey was there.

"How are we doing, honey?" she asked, completely cheerful.

"I don't know. It hurts so bad."

"Okay. Let me check and see how you're coming along."

"I'll wait outside," Marcus said before stepping out of the room.

"Is that the baby's father?" Hailey asked as she checked my

dilation.

"No, he's just a friend."

She finished checking. "You're nearly there. I'm going to call the doctor and let him know."

I nodded as another contraction started. Hailey helped me through it, then left to call the doctor.

Marcus came back in. "How's it going?"

"She said it's almost time to push. The doctor should be here soon."

"Good," he said, looking as relieved as I felt.

By the time the doctor got there I'd had several more excruciating contractions. Though I could tell Marcus was distressed by my pain, he stayed with me the whole time.

"Are you ready to have this baby, Kate?" Doctor Eggleston asked.

"Yes."

"I think I'll wait outside," Marcus murmured to me.

"I'd like you to stay," I said.

"Are you sure?"

"You've been here for the hard parts. You don't want to miss the finale, do you?"

He smiled. "No."

"What's your name, young man?" Doctor Eggleston asked.

"Marcus."

"Okay, I want you to help Kate sit up a bit. And Kate, on the next contraction I want you to push as hard as you can."

With Marcus' help I was able to partially sit up. Hailey and another nurse assisted the doctor. The doctor glanced at the monitor. "Okay, get ready, Kate. And push!"

I strained and pushed as hard as I could.

"Good," Doctor Eggleston said. "Relax for a moment until the next one."

Marcus helped me lay back until the next contraction came. After several pushes, Marcus began to vocally encourage me to push as well.

Finally, about thirty minutes later Doctor Eggleston said, "I see her head, Kate. She's almost here."

Encouraged by the progress, I pushed even harder on the next contraction.

"There's her head," Doctor Eggleston said. "One more push and she'll be out."

During the next contraction I pushed with all my might.

She was out! The pain immediately ended and relief swept over me. A moment later Natalie started wailing.

"Would you like to cut the cord, Marcus?" Doctor Eggleston asked.

Marcus looked at me and I nodded. He took the scissors from the doctor's hand and carefully cut the cord. The nurses cleaned Natalie, cleared her nose and mouth, and wrapped her in a warm blanket before handing her to me. She continued to cry.

"Hi, baby girl," I murmured. At the sound of my voice, she immediately stopped crying. I held her to me, falling in love instantly and completely.

"She's beautiful, Kate," Marcus said, visibly awed by the whole experience.

"She is, isn't she?" I gazed at my new baby daughter. She had a mass of dark hair on her head and her eyes were the same vivid blue as Trevor's.

Trevor, I suddenly thought. He has a right to know his baby has been born. I pushed the thought aside, wanting only to revel in the joy of my new baby girl.

I turned to Marcus. "Thank you so much for being here. You made it so much better."

His incredible green eyes sparkled more than usual as a wide grin lit his face.

"Okay, mommy," the nurse said. "We're going to move you to your room."

A short time later I was settled in my room, Natalie tucked securely in my arms.

"I'm going to take off and let you rest," Marcus said.

"Okay."

"If you want, I can come back later."

I smiled. "I'd like that."

"All right." He leaned over and looked at Natalie. "She's beautiful."

"Thanks."

I watched as he left my room. Then I allowed myself to think about Trevor. I considered when I should tell him his daughter was here.

I'll wait until I'm back home, I decided after only a moment.

CHAPTER THIRTY-NINE

The next day, as I nursed Natalie, I gazed at her and my love for her filled me to overflowing. I never knew I could love another person so much. Snuggling her closer to me, I gazed at her sweet face.

When I heard the door to my hospital room open, I looked up, expecting to see an orderly brining my lunch. Instead I gasped as Trevor walked in the room.

"Trevor. How did you know I was here?"

He walked toward me, his eyes on Natalie. "When you were gone all day, I figured you might be having the baby. And I was right." His eyes met mine and he smiled. "She's so beautiful. Can I hold her?"

Instinctively, my arms tightened around my precious baby girl. "She's eating right now."

"I can see that," he said, watching Natalie nurse.

I pulled the sheet up to cover myself, feeling exposed.

"Oh come on, Lily. It's not like I haven't seen them before."

Ignoring his comment, I adjusted the sheet so I could see Natalie.

Trevor sat in the empty chair next to my bed, making it clear he was in no hurry to leave.

"How did you know I had been gone all day? Have you been watching my house?"

He grinned. "I stopped by to see you and you weren't home. I knew you'd stopped working and I knew it was getting close to your time to have the baby. It wasn't hard to figure out."

"Oh." It sounded reasonable enough. I decided to be civil for all our sakes. "Were you able to find a job?"

"Yes, I was. And an apartment too."

I nodded. "Where are you working?"

"At a shop in town. You wouldn't know where it is."

I wondered if he really even had a job.

Natalie pulled away from my breast and I put her to my shoulder, gently patting her back until she burped.

"Can I hold her now?" Trevor asked eagerly.

I couldn't think of a legitimate reason to tell him no, so I handed her to him. "Make sure and support her head." He surprised me with how comfortable he seemed with her. "Have you held a lot of babies?" I asked.

"Sure," he said, completely confident. "Remember I have all those nieces and nephews. I held them when they were small."

As I realized he was more experienced than me, I suddenly felt inadequate.

"We made a nice-looking kid, Lily." He smiled at me, looking very proud of himself.

Since I agreed completely, I couldn't help but smile back.

Natalie began fussing and I thought Trevor would want to give her back to me, but instead, he expertly placed her against his shoulder and gently bounced her until she settled back down. She snuggled against his shoulder, sleeping, looking totally content. I smiled at the sweet image of the two of them, but felt sad that I couldn't trust Trevor enough to let him into my life as my husband.

Trevor shifted Natalie into his hands, held out in front of him and gazed at her. "I'm so glad I found you, Lily. Now that I've held my daughter, I know I have to be a part of her life."

I stared at him, but he didn't look at me. His gaze was locked on Natalie. Then he turned to me.

"Don't you see now that the three of us need to be together? To be a family?"

I thought about the night a few weeks before when Trevor had come over after he'd obviously been drinking. I pictured his face when Marcus had come down the stairs. And then I recalled how he had moved toward me in a threatening way and probably would have hurt me if Greta hadn't intervened. No, I did not agree that we needed to be a family.

As I looked at him, I tried to think how I could convince him, without upsetting him, that it wasn't going to happen. And I didn't want him holding Natalie while the conversation took place. I held out my hands. "Can I have her back now?"

He seemed reluctant to hand her over, but he finally did.

I laid her against my chest and she continued sleeping. "Trevor, we need to talk," I began.

His chair was facing me and the smile he'd had disappeared. "Okay."

"I know in your mind you're picturing us as this perfect little family, but in reality that's not how it is."

"You're just not seeing the big picture," he interrupted. "You're too focused on the past. You need to look at the future."

I shook my head. "Just a few weeks ago you burst into my house uninvited and scared me with your behavior. Do you remember that?"

"I was just surprised to see your 'friend' there. I didn't mean to scare you."

"But that's just it, Trevor. You never 'mean' to scare me or hurt me, but it happens nonetheless. I refuse to live that way."

"What about me?" he asked.

"What do you mean?"

"Where do I fit in to things? I want to be in Natalie's life. I *am* her father, you know."

"Of course I know that. I guess we'll just have to work out the custody arrangements."

He shook his head and stared at the floor for a minute, then looked back at me. "This is all wrong, Lily. You're talking about divorce and custody like it's nothing. I don't think you even care."

My heart pounded at his accusation. "You think I do this lightly? Do you have any idea how much I've agonized over this? How many chances I've given you? I wanted this to work. I guess you didn't really understand that it was up to you. But time after time you've shown that you can't be trusted to keep yourself under control. I can't live a life where I'm constantly walking on eggshells for fear my husband will find some reason to get angry at me and hurt me." My voice dropped to a whisper. "I just can't do it."

I watched Trevor's reaction. At first he seemed shocked by what I'd said, but as I watched, his expression slowly morphed into anger.

"You act like you had nothing to do with this. Like you're Little Miss Perfect. If only I could be as perfect as you, everything would be fine."

I shook my head, but he ignored me.

"Well, newsflash, Lily. I'm not perfect and I never will be. But at least I'm trying. You're not even willing to try. You're ready to give up at the first challenge. That's not how marriages should work. I know you never saw a marriage up close, but I did. It takes work. I guess you're just not willing to put in the work."

The way he had turned it all around and twisted it to make it look like it was my fault made me furious. I had done everything I knew to make our marriage work, but I wasn't willing to live with a controlling, jealous, abusive husband. He seemed incapable of recognizing his serious faults and I didn't have any hope that he would change. And I didn't have the energy to help him. That was something he'd have to do on his own.

"Trevor, we see things completely differently and I don't think that's going to change. But you know what? That's okay. You can live your life and I can live mine. We just are not going to be living those lives together."

I watched Trevor's face and it seemed like he was beginning to accept what I was saying. But then, like usual, hurt and anger crowded out reason. His eyes narrowed as he spoke.

"Fine, Lily. Have it your way. I'll grant you the divorce. But you'd better believe that I will be in Natalie's life whether you want me to be or not."

For some reason, his words scared me. Even though I hoped he meant what he said about granting the divorce, I wondered what price I would have to pay. Finally he stood to leave. He reached toward Natalie and I instinctively held her tighter.

Trevor sneered at me. "I'm not going to take her. I just want to tell her good-bye."

With trepidation, I handed her to him. He nuzzled her soft head and kissed her. Then he handed her back.

"Thank you," I said.

Just then the door to my room opened and Marcus walked in. Trevor turned to see who had come in, then spun back toward me. "What's *he* doing here?" he asked through clenched teeth.

I felt my face go pale. "He's just a friend, Trevor," I said quietly.

"I'm sorry," Marcus said from the doorway. "I can come back later."

Trevor never looked away from me as he spoke with venom in his voice. "I was just leaving."

As soon as Trevor was gone, I collapsed into tears. Marcus was by my side in seconds.

"Kate, are you okay?"

I nodded, trying to get myself under control.

"Who is that guy?" he asked.

My tears slowed, then stopped. I set Natalie on my legs and grabbed a tissue to blow my nose. Looking at Marcus, I felt he deserved the truth. "He's my husband."

"Your husband?"

I could see the stunned look on his face.

"And I suppose your name really is Lily."

I nodded.

He looked disgusted. "You lied to me?"

"Please. Let me explain."

"You know, that's exactly what Marissa said to me when I told her I'd had enough of her lies."

"I understand you're angry," I quickly interjected. "But I have a good reason."

"Wow. Are all women alike? You're sounding more and more like Marissa with every word." He stood and turned toward the door.

I couldn't let him leave without trying to tell him the circumstances. "Wait, Marcus. You've got to understand. I was hiding from my husband. I couldn't tell anyone."

Before I could finish my explanation, he opened the door. "Yeah, sure. See you around . . . Kate, Lily, whatever."

As the door closed behind him, sobs welled up and I couldn't hold them back. I lifted Natalie from my legs and held her to me. "You won't leave me, will you?" I sobbed.

CHAPTER FORTY

When it was time to check out, I found myself with a problem. I didn't have anyone to drive me home. I considered asking Trish, but I was embarrassed about all that had happened. I even briefly considered calling Trevor, but knew that would just encourage him.

Finally I thought of someone to ask. I grabbed my cell phone and dialed.

"*Billi's* boutique," a cheerful voice answered. "Maddy speaking."

"Maddy," I said, happy to hear a friendly voice. "It's Kate."

"Kate! How are you? Did you have that baby yet?"

"Yes," I said, smiling despite my problems. "In fact, that's why I was calling. The person who was supposed to bring me home from the hospital is not going to be able to do it and I was wondering if you might be available to pick me up and drive me home."

"I'd love to," she said. "I'm off in an hour. Can you wait until then?"

"Yes. Also, the baby's car seat is at home."

"Oh, don't worry. My sister has a baby. I'll swing by and borrow hers."

"Oh, Maddy. You're a life saver. Thank you so much."

"I'm excited to see your baby. You were having a girl, right?"

"Yes. I named her Natalie."

"That's a beautiful name. I can't wait to see her."

I told her my room number, then we hung up. Relieved to have my ride taken care of, I decided to get Natalie ready. First I changed her diaper, which took me longer than I thought it would—I knew it wouldn't take long for me to become an expert though. Then I grabbed the new diaper bag I'd brought and pulled out the cute outfit I'd bought for the occasion. Natalie's bright blue eyes watched me as I struggled to get her arms into the sleeves.

"We want to make sure you're nice and warm," I said to her. Once she was dressed, I sat on the bed and leaned against the pillows. Putting my feet on the bed so my legs were bent, I propped her against my legs so I could gaze at her. Everything she did fascinated me and I knew I could watch her for hours.

When Maddy got there I let her hold the baby while I went through the checkout process. A short time later we were all strapped into the car and on our way home.

"How have things been at the store?" I asked.

"It's been really busy with Christmas so close," Maddy said as she glanced at me then looked back at the road. "We've really missed you."

"Ohh, thanks. That makes me feel good."

"It's true. A lot of the regulars have asked about you and if you've had your baby." She paused. "Hey, I know. Maybe you can take a picture of her and we can put it on the register or something, so that everyone can see." Then she laughed. "That's really old school, isn't it? But a lot of our customers aren't really into Facebook."

"I don't have a Facebook page anyway."

"Really?"

"Yeah," I said, thinking how that could have led Trevor right to me, although in the end it hadn't made a difference.

When we got to my street I directed her to Trish's house. "I need to get my key from my neighbor. She's been feeding my dog."

Maddy pulled up to Trish's house.

"Do you want me to get it?" Maddy asked.

I was still recovering from child birth and couldn't jump out of the car as easily as usual. Not only that, but I was fairly certain Marcus would have told Trish that I had lied about my name and my marital status. I really didn't want to face her. "Yes, thanks."

Maddy walked up to the front door and rang the bell. I saw the door open but couldn't see who had answered. A moment later Maddy was climbing back in the car and handing me my house key.

"Thanks," I said as I tucked it into my purse.

A moment later we pulled up to my house.

"Do you need any help bringing stuff in?" Maddy asked.

"If you want to grab my overnight bag, I can get the baby and her diaper bag."

Within a few minutes we had everything in the house. Greta was ecstatic to see me, her tail wagging harder than I had ever seen it.

"Thanks for bringing me home, Maddy."

"No problem. I'm glad I got to see your beautiful baby."

After she left, I checked Greta's food and water bowls to make sure she had what she needed. Then, with Natalie in my arms, I sat on the couch and called Greta over.

"This is my new baby," I said to her, letting her sniff Natalie. "We need to take good care of her. Okay?"

Greta responded by wagging her tail again. I pet her with my free hand and praised her for being such a good dog.

Natalie began fussing and Greta looked at her, apparently wondering what this new creature was. I took Natalie upstairs and changed her diaper on the new changing table, then sat in the rocking chair and nursed her. When she had finished eating and had been burped, I held her against my shoulder and rocked her. She soon fell asleep.

After placing her in the crib I went into my room and unpacked the things I had taken to the hospital. I could hardly believe my baby was here and that I was no longer pregnant. I looked at myself in the mirror and saw that my belly was still large. I knew it would take several weeks for my uterus to shrink back to normal, but I was impatient to get back into shape.

Once things were organized, I made sure the burglar alarm was set, then lay on my bed and took a nap. It felt good to be in my own bed again after being in the hospital. I slept soundly, but woke abruptly when I heard Natalie crying. Pushing myself off of my bed, I went into her room and stood next to the crib, gazing at her. She was so perfect. Her tiny fists waved in the air as she cried and I laughed as her perfect little mouth occasionally turned down into a frown. I reached in and scooped her up, then held her against me. Though her cries weren't as loud, she still fussed and I assumed she was hungry.

I sat on the rocking chair and began nursing her. She ate hungrily. Powerful waves of love cascaded over me as I watched her. I stroked her head with my free hand and was amazed by her soft hair. When she was satisfied, I changed her diaper and brought her downstairs.

I had bought a baby seat and had placed it on the dining room table. After placing her in it, I fixed myself something to eat, then sat near her and ate my meal. I had only been a mother for a very short period of time, but already I loved it.

I was extremely grateful for the money I had from Dad's life insurance policy as well as the sale of his house, which allowed me to be home with Natalie. I knew I would need to continue with my classes as soon as possible, perhaps some Web-based classes, but for the time being I would enjoy taking care of her full-time.

Before Natalie was born I had made the time to finalize the website for *Billi's* boutique. Two of the other business owners had also wanted me to create websites for them, which I had done. So now I just needed to maintain the websites until I was ready to look for additional clients. Running my own business, even though it was so small, was very exciting and bolstered my self-confidence. The extra income I earned helped me to feel secure as I cared for Natalie and adjusted to being a mom.

Over the next few days I was able to get in to a loose routine.

Natalie had her own schedule, but things were coming together. Though I didn't have any visitors, I didn't feel quite as lonely with Natalie and Greta always there. But when Natalie was about a week old, Trevor stopped by. In a way I was glad to see him. It had been so quiet with just Natalie, Greta and me, I didn't mind that he had come over.

As soon as I invited him in, he wanted to see Natalie.

"She's sleeping, but I guess I can get her," I said.

"I'd appreciate that."

I went into her room and picked her up from her crib, then brought her down and handed her to Trevor.

"She's so tiny," he said as he held her.

I watched him with her and again felt impressed with his confidence. Some men were scared to hold newborns, afraid they might hurt them, but Trevor obviously knew what he was doing.

He gently bounced her in his arms, with his hands held out in front of him so he could watch her. After a moment, her eyes cracked open and she yawned so big that it made her cry. Trevor laughed and she quickly settled back down.

He looked at her open eyes. "I think she has my eyes." He looked at me. "What do you think, Lily?"

I nodded, a feeling of warmth for him settling in my heart. "Yes, she does. I hope they stay that color."

"Me too," he said, gazing at her once again. After a moment he put her against his shoulder and looked at me. "How are you doing, Lily? Do you need anything?"

I was touched by his concern. No one else had checked on me or asked about my needs. "I'm doing okay. She sleeps pretty well at night, about four hours at a time, so I'm able to get enough sleep."

"What about groceries? Have you been able to get to the store?"

"Not yet. In fact I was thinking about going later today."

"Do you want me to stay here and take care of her while you go?"

he asked, looking eager to have time alone with his baby.

I wasn't ready to give him that kind of access to Natalie or my home. "No, that's okay," I quickly said, then felt bad at the look of rejection on his face. "It's just that I'm not ready to be away from her yet."

He stared at me, apparently trying to decide what to say. Finally he said, "I've hardly spent any time with her. You've never been away from her."

"I understand that, Trevor. But in some ways it's different for the mother. I carried her inside me for nine months and went through an agonizing birth to get her here. I nurse her at my breast every few hours." I shook my head. "It's not the same."

He nodded, seeming reluctant to agree. "Yeah, I guess I see what you mean. But I would like to spend more time with her. How is she going to know me unless I see her more often?"

"She's so little now—I don't know how much she notices who is with her yet."

"Still, it needs to start at the beginning."

"What did you have in mind?"

"I was thinking of coming by two or three days a week."

The thought of him coming so often was unnerving, but I didn't feel like it was up to me to refuse. There was no court order and I really didn't want to get the courts involved at this point. If we could keep our relationship civil, it would be so much better. "How about on Mondays and Thursdays?"

"Okay. Let's try that and see how it works out."

I smiled, relieved he wasn't going to push for three days a week.

"Maybe you can use that time to run errands or something. You know, have some time to yourself," he said.

"I'll have to think about that."

He nodded, apparently pleased with my response.

After an hour, Natalie began fussing. Trevor handed her back to me. With her in my arms, I stood and gently bounced her, but she was making it clear she was hungry.

"I think I'm going to have to feed her. Maybe this is a good time for you to go." I didn't want to be rude or mean, but I wasn't about to have him watch me nurse her again. I hadn't liked it in the hospital and there was no reason for him to stay and watch me now.

"Sure, okay." He stood and walked to the door. "I'll be back on Thursday. Probably in the late afternoon. Is that okay?"

I nodded, happy he was asking me and not just telling me. "Sounds good."

After he left I was able to feed Natalie and put her back down for a nap. As I watched her sleep in her crib, I thought about Trevor and found I was actually glad he wanted to be part of her life. It would be good for her to have both of us loving her and caring for her. We just needed to try to get along and it would all work out.

CHAPTER FORTY-ONE

Christmas came and went. Beyond putting up the tree, this year I didn't have the energy or the interest to do the whole Christmas celebration. Thankfully, Trevor's day to visit didn't fall on Christmas, so I was able to focus on my new little family on that day and just relax and enjoy being with Natalie.

Over the next few weeks Trevor stuck to our prearranged schedule and it was working out well. I hadn't taken him up on his offer for me to run errands while he stayed with Natalie, but I was beginning to feel more comfortable with having him around. A few times he'd brought up the subject of us getting back together, but when I asked him to stop asking me, he'd respected my request.

When Natalie was six weeks old, he came over at the appointed time and we sat on the couch like usual. I had tried to feed her before he came so that she wouldn't get hungry while he was playing with her, but she wasn't hungry yet. When Trevor had been there for forty-five minutes, she began to get fussy.

"Sorry, Trevor. I tried to feed her earlier, but she wasn't hungry."

"It sure would be nice if I could feed her," he said, trying to get her to take a pacifier.

I laughed. "Well, you don't exactly have the right equipment."

He smiled. "I know. But I could always give her formula."

"No," I said, maybe a bit too emphatically. "I mean, that would mess up my milk production if she had formula instead of nursing."

"Oh. Well, it was just a thought."

I watched the two of them interact. At first the pacifier had satisfied her, but pretty soon it wasn't enough and she began to cry.

Trevor handed her back to me. "Since I can't do anything about feeding her, and you don't want to feed her in front of me, maybe you should let me know when she's eaten and I came come over earlier or later so that she doesn't get hungry while I'm here."

I could tell he was irritated with me—like he thought I had done this on purpose. Controlling my annoyance, I nodded. "That's fine."

He stood abruptly and grabbed his coat off the chair. "I guess I'll see you Monday." He jammed his arms through the sleeves of his coat.

I didn't respond as he stomped out the door, nearly slamming it as he left. As soon as I heard him drive away, I locked the door and turned on the burglar alarm, then I settled onto the couch and nursed Natalie.

An hour later I heard a knock on the door and felt my heart race as I imagined Trevor returning. Natalie was sleeping in her crib and I didn't want to have to take a chance on waking her up to let Trevor hold her. I peeked through the blinds, but didn't see Trevor's car.

"Who could that be?" I asked Greta as she barked a few times at the door.

I peered through the peephole and was surprised to see Marcus standing on my porch. Opening the door, I smiled tentatively, wondering why he had come over.

"Hi, Marcus."

"Hey. How are you?"

"I'm doing okay."

"You look good," he said, glancing at my stomach, which was nearly back to its pre-pregnancy flatness.

"Thanks," I smiled at his compliment. "Do you want to come in?"

"If you're not busy."

"No, I was just reading."

He followed me to the couch and we sat on opposite sides.

"How's the baby?" he asked.

My smile widened. "She's great. She's asleep right now, but if you want, you can go look at her."

"Okay."

We walked up the stairs and entered Natalie's room. He went to the crib and stared down at her.

"She's as beautiful as I remember," he whispered.

I nodded. "She's getting bigger too."

He looked at me. "It was really cool being there when she was born. I don't think I'll ever forget that."

I smiled. "I was really glad you were there."

He looked at Natalie again, then back at me. "Can we talk?"

My smile diminished. "Sure. Let's go back downstairs."

He nodded and followed me back down. Once we were on the couch, I waited for him to begin. I was certain this was about the lies I'd told him and I could feel the tension in the room.

"I'm sorry I reacted like I did in your hospital room," he said.

"It's not your fault," I quickly assured him.

"Yes, it is. You had just had a baby and I got mad at you and wouldn't listen to you when you were at your most vulnerable. I was just thinking about myself and how I felt." He paused and I waited to see what else he wanted to say. "Ever since that day I've been thinking about you and what you said. You said something about hiding from your husband and then I thought about the self-defense lessons you wanted me to teach you and I started putting it together and realized you were telling the truth."

"I'm sorry I couldn't tell you before. I just didn't want to take the chance on Trevor finding me."

"But he did find you."

"Yes, he did. Despite my best efforts."

"So are you going to get back together with him?"

"Oh no," I said without hesitation. "Not a chance."

"Do you mind my asking how he feels about that?"

"No, that's okay. I haven't had anyone to talk to about this, so I'm glad to talk to you."

"So you've been doing this all on your own?"

"Well, yeah. I thought you knew that."

His face reddened. "I guess I assumed you had other people to turn to. I feel even worse now."

"Don't, Marcus. It's not your fault. And I've discovered I'm a lot stronger than I thought I was."

"Can I ask why you left this guy?"

Even though Marcus was my friend, I didn't want to get in to all the details. "Well, I'll put it this way. He wasn't the man I thought I had married."

"Okay. Based on the fact that you got Greta and took self-defense classes, I can only assume you were afraid of him."

I nodded, willing to confirm the obvious.

"What about now? Has he been bothering you?"

"Not exactly. I mean, he wants to see Natalie and I've been letting him come over two days a week and play with her. It's been going fine." I thought to earlier that evening and how he had stomped off like a toddler throwing a tantrum and wondered how much longer he'd be happy with me constantly supervising his visits. But I wasn't ready to leave Natalie with him. Maybe next time I can leave him alone in the room while I do some cleaning, I thought.

"I guess I can see why he was so mad when he saw me here that night."

I raised my eyebrows briefly in a gesture of *That's what I expected of him.* "Jealousy is one of his problems."

"Oh." He paused. "I should probably get going. But I just wanted to come over and say I'm sorry for how I reacted."

"I appreciate that, Marcus."

He seemed to hesitate.

"What?" I asked.

"Do you want me to call you Kate or Lily?"

I laughed a little, embarrassed to have such a question asked. "Lily, I guess. That's my real name. Now that Trevor's found me, there's really no reason to use Kate."

He smiled. "Lily. I like the sound of it."

He stood and I walked him to the door. "Feel free to stop by anytime." I paused. "Unless there's a blue Camaro here, that is."

"Okay."

"He usually comes over on Monday and Thursday evenings."

"I'll keep that in mind. I'll see you later. Lily."

I liked the way my name sounded coming from him. "Bye, Marcus."

CHAPTER FORTY-TWO

The next time Trevor came over I asked if it would be okay if I did some cleaning while he was taking care of Natalie.

"Yeah, go right ahead." He held Natalie close to his face. "We'll be fine."

I felt happy as I watched them. Natalie was starting to smile occasionally and I hoped she would smile for Trevor. I knew he would be thrilled if she did. I left them in the living room and got out my cleaning supplies, taking them to the upstairs bathroom. I gave the bathroom a good scrubbing, then worked on the half bath downstairs. On the way to the half bath I glanced at Trevor and Natalie and they were doing fine.

When I was done with the bathrooms, I scrubbed the kitchen sink, then got some dust rags and cleaned all the dusty surfaces in the house. Then I used the special broom/mop I had gotten for wood floors and cleaned all the floors.

By the time I was done it was the end of Trevor's visit. I went back in to the living room to see how they were doing. Trevor was rocking Natalie in his arms and she was drifting off to sleep. He smiled at me as I came in the room.

"Did you ever know you could love someone so much?" he asked.

I smiled back. "No. It's a special kind of love, isn't it?" I walked toward the two of them, ready to take Natalie. When I stopped next to them, Trevor used his free arm to pull me close to him.

"We need to be a family, Lily," he said with intensity. "How can

Christine Kersey

you deny it?"

With him holding Natalie, I didn't want to push him away. His grip was strong and I couldn't easily get any distance without risking him dropping the baby.

"Trevor, you're hurting me. Let go."

His grip only became tighter. "I can't let you go. Don't you see? I *need* you."

"Trevor, stop it," I said in my most commanding voice.

Our conversation woke Natalie and she started crying.

"See what you've done?" he said. "You've woken my baby."

The way he said it made alarm bells ring in my head. "Let me have her."

"It's all about you, isn't it, Lily? It's always all about you. Well, I'm tired of always having to go along with what you want. Now it's time for me to have things my way."

He still had his right arm wrapped tightly around me and Natalie held in his left. I knew I could get free if I used the self-defense moves I'd practiced, but there was a risk he would drop Natalie and I didn't want to take that chance.

"What do you mean? What is it you want?"

"Well, Lily, my first choice is to have you as my wife. But since you keep being so stubborn about that, I'll have to go with my second option."

I could only guess what he had in mind. My heart pounded as I imagined what he meant and I felt my heart rate increase. As blood pounded through my ears my vision began to narrow and my ears began to ring. I remembered learning in my self-defense class that if my heart rate kept increasing, I would soon lose my fine motor control. My gross motor control would go next and I would be rendered helpless, not able to do anything but swing my arms uselessly from side to side. To keep that from happening, I needed to take a deep breath. I tried to, but Trevor's arm was wrapped so tightly around me that I

236

couldn't fill my lungs. I did the best I could and I started to feel marginally better.

Greta had come into the room while this was going on and seemed unsure what to do. She couldn't get to Trevor as long as I was pressed up against him and Natalie was in his arms, so she stayed in place, watching.

Trevor apparently noticed her watching him. "You need to put that dog outside, Lily."

I hoped that would give me the opening I needed to somehow get my baby back. "Okay, but you'll have to let go of me."

His grip slackened, but he still held on. "I'm not going to let go. I'll just walk with you."

I took a step toward the back door, forcing air into my lungs at the same time.

He spoke into my ear. "Remember who's holding the baby."

I felt my face pale and stopped walking, then turned toward him as much as I could with his iron grip on my arm. "Please don't hurt her," I barely managed to say, as I felt the fear choke me.

"I would never hurt her."

I didn't understand what he had meant and wanted to ask him, but he pulled on my arm.

"Just get that dog outside," he said.

I took small steps toward the back door and Greta followed.

"Put that plastic thing in the dog door."

I did as instructed.

"Now open the door and let her out."

"Okay." I was too scared to disobey, not knowing what he might do to Natalie. "Come on, Greta," I said, opening the back door and encouraging her to go outside. She seemed hesitant, but I kept encouraging her until she went out.

Trevor closed the door before I had a chance to. "That's better," he said.

He let go of my arm and I spun toward him. The way he was acting was like the Trevor I'd run away from in Reno, and I was scared. I looked at Natalie, crying in his arms, and didn't know what to do. My self-defense lessons had never involved a baby. "What do you want?"

"You've had your turn with Natalie since she was born. Now it's my turn to have her."

As the meaning of his words sunk in, I felt a scream climbing up my throat. I opened my mouth and took a breath, but before I could make a sound, Trevor swung his fist toward my head so swiftly that I didn't have time to react. As his fist made contact, I thought my head would explode. Stars appeared before my eyes and I started blacking out. I felt myself falling in what felt like slow motion. I could hear Greta barking frantically outside the back door, but it sounded muffled. Finally everything went black as I fell to the floor, unconscious.

CHAPTER FORTY-THREE

When I woke up, my hands were tied behind my back, my ankles were tied together, and I was lying on the ground, my cheek pressed against the wood floor. I was still by the back door where I had fallen, but Greta had stopped barking. At first I was groggy and couldn't remember exactly what had happened, but as the fog cleared from my mind, it all came back to me in stunning detail.

"Natalie," I whispered, as I understood that Trevor had taken her. No more words came out of my mouth as the reality of what had happened pressed down upon me and seemed to crush my very soul. Heartbreaking sobs rose to the surface from the deepest part of me, and I lay there, a puddle of tears forming on the floor under my cheek.

The grief overwhelmed me and I wanted to die. I couldn't go on without my baby girl. She was such an integral part of my life now that I couldn't see myself living without her. As I pictured her sweet face, my breasts ached as milk filled the ducts. It was time to feed her and my body knew it.

How would Trevor care for her? She had never used a bottle before. Would she be able to? How would she react to the formula he was sure to give her? Anger pounded through my body as I pictured him knocking me down, tying me up, then running off with my baby. He had no right. Was he doing it just to hurt me? I had seen him with her and he had always been tender, but he had never had to deal with her when she was upset. Would be able to take care of her properly?

I had to get her back.

With difficulty, I managed to get myself into a sitting position. Then, scooting backward until my back was against the wall, I pushed against it and was able to stand. I hopped into the kitchen and turned my back to one of the drawers. Using my hands, I pulled the drawer open and carefully felt around until I found a pair of scissors.

Though my wrists were tied, I could move my hands and I was able to open the scissors. I set the scissor handle over the front of the drawer, causing the sharp part of the open scissors to point upward, then pushed the drawer closed, which held the scissors in place.

Then I put the rope against the sharp edge of the scissors and carefully, so as not to make the scissors fall over, I rubbed the rope against the sharp edge. Time seemed to stop as I slowly sawed the rope against the scissors. Finally it felt like the ropes were loosening. Then, one of the layers of rope broke.

I took a deep breath, forcing myself to be patient and continued my task. Eventually the ropes loosened enough that I was able to get my hands free. Tears pushed into my eyes in relief. Blinking rapidly to clear my vision, I bent to my ankles and tried to untie the rope. My hands shook and I was having trouble getting the knot loose. Grabbing the scissors, I cut at the rope until I was free.

I looked at the clock and realized it had been nearly an hour since Trevor had knocked me out and tied me up. My first instinct was to call the police, but then I remembered the money I'd hidden in the secret room and wondered if I could use it to lure Trevor back. I had no idea where he'd gone, but I did have his cell phone number.

Racing to my purse, I pulled out my cell phone and punched in his number. Not surprisingly, he didn't answer. I listened for his the beep and then left a voice message.

"Trevor, I know you have Natalie," my voice shook and I took a deep breath to gain control. "You might be interested to know that I have something you might want. I found the SD card in your gym bag before I mailed it back to you and I dug up the money. I'll make a trade with you. If you bring Natalie back, I'll give you the two-hundred thousand dollars."

I hung up, then went to the back door and let Greta in. She burst through the door, agitated. I was certain she could sense that something was very wrong.

"It will be okay," I murmured as I knelt next to her and hugged her.

I paced as I waited for him to call back. After ten minutes I couldn't take it anymore. I called Marcus' cell phone. He didn't answer. "Marcus, please call me as soon as you get this." I felt myself losing control. My voice shook and I forced myself to speak slowly or Marcus would never understand what I said. "Trevor took Natalie."

I hung up and walked into the living room, setting my cell phone on the coffee table, then looked out the window. It was almost dark outside but I stared out, hoping somehow that Trevor would decide to bring Natalie back.

After several minutes I knew my hopes were just a fantasy. He had no intention of bringing her back. I wasn't even sure if the money would lure him here. As the last bit of hope seeped out of my heart, I collapsed on the couch.

The image of Natalie in Trevor's arms, crying and hungry, filled my mind. Would he know what to do to care for her? What if he gets upset and hurts her? As I imagined the worse, panic engulfed me. Hysteria climbed up my throat and uncontrollable sobs pushed their way out of my mouth.

I lay there, a slave to my emotions. Tears and snot ran down my face, but I didn't care. All I could think about was my baby and never seeing her again. The thought that I had seen Natalie for the last time threw me into fresh hysterics. I felt myself falling into an abyss. I was sinking, sinking. I welcomed the black wave that was slowly drowning me. I didn't want to live if I couldn't have my baby with me.

My cell phone rang. The sound slowly pulled me above the wave.

It felt like a life preserver. I lifted myself from the couch and wiped my eyes and nose on my sleeve, then reached for the cell phone on the coffee table.

"Hello?" my voice cracked.

"Lily?"

My hopes soared. It was Trevor. I heard Natalie crying in the background and I dissolved into tears. "Please, Trevor. Please bring her back."

"Lily, you know I can't do that. You and I both know I've crossed a line and if you get her back you'll run again. I can't let you take my baby away from me."

"Trevor, I'm begging you," I said, sobbing. "I'll do anything. I'll stay married to you if that's what you want. Just bring her back."

"Your lies won't fool me. I know you'll say anything at this point to get her back. I know it's over between us. I gave you so many chances to come back to me and you turned down each and every one. You know, Lily, it's funny. Amanda can't have children, but she said she's always wanted to be a mother. I promised her that if it didn't work out between you and me that I'd get her a baby." His voice softened. "My baby."

"No!" I screamed. *This is just a nightmare. I'll wake up and Natalie will be in her crib.* Frantically, I pinched my arm, trying to wake up. When that didn't work I started hyperventilating. I began blacking out. Desperately, I took a deep breath. I couldn't break this connection with Trevor. I had to convince him to bring Natalie back.

"You know, Lily, you were my first choice. I had to be sure it was really over before I decided on Amanda. But you made it perfectly clear that you didn't want me. It's too bad, really. We could have made lots of beautiful babies together."

Desperate for a way to get Natalie back before Trevor disappeared with her, my mind raced. "Trevor," I hurriedly said. "Did you get my message? About the money?"

"Yes, but you know I can't believe you."

"I have it! I have it!" I screamed, frantic for him to believe me. "I don't even want it! I was waiting to give it back to you!"

He laughed. "Lily, take a breath."

Tears ran down my face as I sobbed. "It's in a metal box. I had to use bolt cutters to open it. I put the rocks back after I dug it up."

Trevor was silent and for a moment and I thought I'd lost the connection. Then I heard Natalie fussing in the background.

"How did you know where to find it?" he asked.

He's starting to believe me! "On the SD card. There was a file. It had the GPS coordinates. I used the coordinates to find it. I had to walk around before I found the pile of rocks."

"You little . . .," Trevor said. "Okay, so you have it. Now what?"

The sliver of hope overwhelmed me and I felt dizzy. I took another deep breath, trying to clear my head. "Come back to the house. I'll give you the money. I don't want it. I just want Natalie."

"No, I have a better idea. We'll meet somewhere and make the exchange."

"Okay," I said, ready to agree to anything. "When and where?"

"Wow. I didn't know you'd be so eager to see me."

"When and where, Trevor. Just tell me and I'll be there."

"Fifteen minutes. The park at the south end of town."

"Okay," I said, but he'd already hung up.

CHAPTER FORTY-FOUR

I put my phone in my purse and grabbed my keys, then raced up the stairs. Greta followed me as I ran into Natalie's room. I tried not to look at Natalie's empty crib as I opened the closet and moved the boxes out of the way. I opened the door to the hidden room and crawled inside.

Frantically, I tossed everything out of the box where I'd stashed the money. Finally I reached the metal box and pulled it out. I had never gotten around to getting a new lock and I had to use two hands to carry it to keep the lid from opening and the money from spilling out.

I sprinted down the stairs, glanced at my purse on the table, but left it there since it would be difficult to grab it with my hands full, and ran out to my car. I was in too much of a hurry to even bother locking the front door. I knew Greta would keep it safe. It was pitch black outside, but the porch light threw enough illumination for me to see what I was doing. Popping open the trunk, I set the metal box inside, then slammed the lid shut before climbing in the driver's seat and turning on the engine.

I threw the car into reverse and spun around until I was facing back down the gravel drive. Spinning my wheels until my tires gained traction, I punched the gas pedal and raced down the drive, turning toward town once I reached the paved street.

Ten minutes later I pulled up to the park and stopped in the only place where there was some light, although it was dim. I didn't see

Trevor's car anywhere. My eyes combed the area, searching for any sign of Trevor and Natalie, but I couldn't see anything in the near-dark. Suddenly I became aware that the front of my shirt was soaked. I wasn't sure if it was from tears or leaking breast milk. Most likely both. I pulled some tissues from the box I kept in the car and blew my nose so I could breath normally.

Five minutes passed and I was starting to feel panicked that he wasn't going to show up, but I knew him well enough to know that he would want that money. As I gazed around the area, I saw a pair of headlights on the other end of the park. The car looked like it was pulling to a stop. The headlights turned off.

Frozen in my seat, I waited to see if Trevor and Natalie would appear from that direction. After several minutes I saw a lone figure walking toward me, a bag over his shoulder. There were a few lights in the area—just enough so that I could see it was Trevor. But he didn't have Natalie with him. Where was she?

Pulling my keys out of the ignition, I climbed out of the car and ran toward him.

"Where is she?! Where is she?!"

"Calm down, Lily. She's in my car."

"You left her alone?"

"She'll be fine. Now where's the money?"

"Bring me Natalie first."

"No. First I need to make sure you have the money."

I had no desire to keep the money so I was willing to go along with his request. "It's in the trunk."

We walked back to my car.

As we entered the dimly lit area, Trevor stopped and looked at me. "Wow, Lily. You're a mess."

Ignoring him, I inserted my key into the trunk and raised the lid. I watched Trevor as he lifted the top on the metal box and touched the money inside.

"It's all there," I said. "I never spent any of it."

He glanced at me. "Good for you. Now put the money in this bag." He handed me his gym bag, the same one where I'd found the SD card. Now I was glad I had taken the money. Without it I wouldn't have had any leverage to get Trevor to meet me and give Natalie back.

I took the bag from him and began transferring the money from the metal box to the gym bag. It didn't take long to move it all over. I handed him the bag. "Okay. Now I want Natalie."

He set the bag down and laughed. "Now I have the money *and* the baby."

My heart dropped. He had no intention of giving Natalie back to me. I glanced at the gym bag. Why had he set it on the ground? Was he planning on attacking me?

Frantically, I ran through the self-defense moves in my head. I tried to be subtle as I got into a defensive stance.

Trevor grinned at me. "I'm sorry we couldn't work it out, Lily. We had a good thing going for a while there. But like all good things, this must come to an end."

He lunged for me, his arms outstretched. But I was ready for him. I put my hands up and deflected his attempt. Then he grabbed my wrists, but I twisted my arms towards his thumbs and broke loose. I glanced around, hopeful that someone would come by, but it was late and no one appeared.

In the moment I looked around, he took advantage of the distraction and put his hands around my neck, trying to strangle me. I put my right arm up in the air and quickly twisted to the side, forcing his hands off my neck. My elbow was bent now and I thrust it at his face, hard. His head snapped back. I lifted my knee and rammed it into his groan. He collapsed to the ground. As he writhed on the grass I felt his pockets and found his keys, then pulled them out and raced toward his car.

As I approached, I could hear Natalie wailing. My hands shook as

I tried to jam the key into the lock. Finally, I was able to unlock the door. As I slid into the driver's seat I glanced back toward Trevor and saw him trying to get up. I shoved the key into the ignition and the engine turned over. Trevor was stumbling in my direction, but I threw the car into reverse and pulled out of the parking space.

I didn't know where to go. I didn't have any money on me and I had left my purse at home. I decided to drive there, get my purse and then drive away. As we headed home, Natalie settled down, the motion of the car rocking her to sleep. Ten minutes later I pulled up to my house.

I thought about Trevor and what he would do next. Would he try to take Natalie again? No doubt he would. At least he won't be able to follow me without a car, I thought. Then the blood drained from my face as I realized the keys to my car had been left in the trunk lock.

He was probably only minutes behind me. Frantically, I tried to figure out what to do. Then it came to me. *The hidden room.* I'll take Natalie and hide in there.

With shaking hands I took her out of her car seat. It was not the car seat from my car. Obviously this was something Trevor had planned ahead of time. I stepped onto the porch and was thankful I hadn't bothered to lock the front door when I'd run out or I wouldn't have a way to get in now.

I carried Natalie into the house and locked the door behind me. Greta greeted me with her usual joy. I wondered what I should do with her. If I brought her into the hidden room she might bark and give our location away. But if I left her in the house, she might stand outside the closet and bark, again giving our location away. As much as I didn't like it, I decided to put her outside.

"Come on, girl," I said as I hurried her to her dog door. "Go on out back." She went out her dog door and I dropped the plastic shield in place. She barked, not liking to be kept outside when I was inside.

I raced to the staircase, then realized I hadn't set the alarm. As I reached toward the buttons, my gaze went to the panic button on the panel. That would call the police right away. Breathing a sigh of relief, I pressed the red button. Nothing happened. A bad feeling swelled within my gut as I pressed the button several times with the same result. Maybe I need to punch in the code first, I thought, frantically pressing the buttons for my security code.

There was no beeping response.

Trevor must have disabled the alarm when I was unconscious, I thought, trying to keep complete panic from taking over. How had he gotten the code? Had he found it when I was unconscious? Had he planned on coming back even after he'd taken Natalie? Why? What was he planning on doing?

Then I heard the crunch of gravel as a car pulled into the drive. Turning to the front door, I jammed my eye to the peephole and saw my car driving toward the house. I was certain Trevor was behind the wheel. With Natalie in my arms, I raced up the stairs to her room and into her closet. I slid the closet door closed, then crawled into the hidden room, Natalie held in one arm. It was awkward, but I was able to do it. Once inside, I set her on the hard floor, then with shaking hands I reached out into the closet and did my best to pull the boxes against the small door as I closed it, hoping it would disguise the door.

I peered out the window and saw my Honda parked out front, but I didn't see Trevor. Terror surged over me in waves as I strained to listen for any indication of what he was doing.

Natalie started fussing. I was sure she must be hungry. I picked her up from the floor, then sat on the ground and leaned against the wall. I lifted my shirt and put her to my breast. She ate hungrily. But most importantly, she was silent.

Suddenly I heard the front door crash open. Tears filled my eyes as I held Natalie against me. Paralyzing panic held me in place as I waited for Trevor to find me.

"Lily, where are you?" Trevor said from somewhere below me.

It sounded like he was searching the first floor.

Moments later I heard a creak on the stairs and knew he was coming.

Frozen with dread, I was terrified about what he would do if he found me. When I heard him walk into the baby's room, I found I couldn't breathe as the horror of my situation overwhelmed me. I prayed Natalie wouldn't make any noise. I heard the floor boards creak as he walked around the room. Then I heard the closet door slide open. I held perfectly still, waiting for him to throw open the door to my sanctuary, but miraculously it didn't sound like he was moving the boxes.

When I heard his footsteps walk away, relief cascaded over me and waves of dizziness made my ears buzz.

"Where are you, Lily? Come out of hiding," he demanded.

It sounded like he had gone into my bedroom.

"I want Natalie back," he said.

I held her closer and looked down at her. She had fallen asleep.

"It will be better if I don't have to track you down. Now come out."

I could tell he was getting agitated. Once he realized we weren't hiding in my bedroom, what would he do? Would he start a more thorough search and find the hidden room? What would I do if he found Natalie?

I knew I had to keep him away from my baby. Doing the only thing I could think of to protect her, I set her on the floor. Even though the floor was hard, she stayed asleep. Then I went to the small door and slowly pushed it open. I crawled out, then closed the door and put the boxes securely against it. I tiptoed out of the closet and pressed myself against the wall. Trevor was still in my bedroom.

"Where are you, Lily?" I heard him roar.

I was hesitant to leave Natalie alone in the room, but in my panicked state I didn't know what else to do. Suddenly I heard the faint sound of Natalie waking. I had to draw Trevor downstairs and I had to do it now. I sprinted down the stairs, purposely making noise.

A moment later I heard him pounding down the stairs behind me. I had barely reached the living room when he caught up to me. I noticed the front door hanging open and the dark night beyond. Then I turned to face him.

"There you are, Lily. Where's my baby?" He stood about five feet away.

"You can't have her," I said. I felt tears threatening, but took a deep breath to get myself under control.

"It's not up to you." He took a step toward me.

"Stop!" I yelled, as I'd been taught in class.

He laughed. "You think you can keep me from my baby?"

"She belongs to both of us," I said, trying to sound reasonable. "Why can't we share custody?"

"Because, as you've so recently demonstrated, you get to set all the rules. I don't like your rules."

I wanted to draw him out of the house and away from Natalie before she began to cry loud enough for him to hear. I turned to run out of the house, but before I took more than two steps, he had locked his arm around my neck. I realized I had broken a cardinal rule of self-defense: Never turn your back on your attacker.

I found it hard to breathe. Using both of my hands, I grabbed the inside of his elbow and yanked, allowing my airway to open. He held on and I swung my head back as hard as I could, hitting his face. He let go with a grunt of surprise. I spun around and saw his nose gushing blood.

He came at me again, a look of fury on his face. I got into a defensive stance with my arms up, bent at the elbow, one hand further forward than the other. He reached for me, but I used my arms to deflect his attempt. He tried again and this time I shot my arm out and pushed his chest. He stumbled backward a few steps, but didn't fall.

Pure hatred glowed in his eyes and I knew he would kill me if I didn't stop him. Fresh adrenaline pulsed through me at the realization and I took a deep breath. This time when he rushed me, he tackled me. I fell to the ground on my back with him on top of me.

"Now we'll see who wins," he said as his hands wrapped around my throat and began to squeeze.

I tried to turn my head to loosen his grasp, but his grip was too tight. Then I tried to move my arms, but realized he was using his knees to pin them against my sides. I tried kicking him with my legs, but he was sitting too far forward for me to reach him.

Blackness filled my peripheral vision. Natalie's face flashed in my mind and utter sadness filled me when I realized she would grow up without a mother as I had. I felt myself fading away but my eyes remained open. Suddenly a flash of fur flew across my limited field of vision and a great weight was lifted from my chest. Trevor was off of me. I took in deep gasps of air as I heard him scream. I managed to turn my head and I saw Greta on top of him, her jaw clamped on his neck. Abruptly, his voice went silent.

I lay there, trying to recover from my near strangulation. Then I slowly sat up and looked around, trying to understand what had happened. The front door was smashed in, Trevor was on the floor, dead or severely injured, Greta had her powerful jaws still around his neck. This time no tears came. I was in shock.

Finally, Greta let go and came and sat by me. I crawled over to Trevor and pressed my fingers against his neck. I didn't feel a pulse. I was surprised that there wasn't very much blood.

"Lily," a voice called from the door.

I swung my head around and saw Marcus standing there.

"I just got your message," he said as he came to me. "What happened?"

Seeing him there made me feel safe and I burst into tears. "He took Natalie," I sobbed, my voice scratchy from Trevor's chokehold.

Panic filled his face. "Where is she?"

"She's fine now," I assured him, through my tears. "But Trevor," I said, motioning down at him. "I think he's . . ."

Marcus checked for a pulse, then looked at me and shook his head. "I think she crushed his windpipe."

"We'd better call the police," I said, trying to stand. Marcus helped me up. I went to the coffee table where I'd left my purse, took out my cell phone, and dialed 911. When someone answered, I tried to explain what had happened. The person on the phone said an officer would be there shortly and had me stay on the phone with her until the officer arrived.

While I was waiting, I took Greta into my bedroom and closed the door, not wanting her to get in the way while everything was going on.

Chapter Forty Five

Within five minutes two police cars and an ambulance had pulled up to the house and I hung up the phone. The emergency personnel first tended to Trevor, but it was obvious he was beyond help. Then they turned to me. Besides the red marks on my neck, I had a good-sized lump on the side of my head where Trevor had hit me. After they checked me, I declined to be taken to the hospital and the ambulance left.

The police officers turned to me, questioning me about what had happened.

"Before we talk, I need to get my baby," I said.

The officers followed me upstairs. I could hear Natalie crying as I got closer to her room. The officers watched as I moved the boxes in the closet out of the way and crawled into the hidden room. One of them followed me in. I picked Natalie up from the floor and handed her out to the officer who was in the outer room, then I crawled out. The other officer followed behind me.

Once Natalie was back in my arms, she settled down.

As we stood in the baby's room I recounted the events of the evening, starting with Trevor knocking me unconscious and tying me up, ending with him strangling me and Greta saving my life. They took careful notes, then told me a detective was on his way.

We went downstairs to wait for the detective to arrive, but with Trevor's body still on the living room floor, the officers suggested we wait in the kitchen. I quickly agreed.

The officers turned to Marcus. "What is your involvement in this?"

"Lily left a message on my cell phone earlier in the evening telling me that Trevor had taken the baby," Marcus said.

"Is that message still on your phone?"

"Yes," he answered as he pulled out his phone and played the message for them.

Marcus put it on speakerphone and it was obvious that I was near hysteria when I'd left the message. Hearing my voice, the emotions slammed into me and I held Natalie tighter.

"And when did you arrive here?" the officer asked Marcus.

"Right before she called you."

"Where were you before that?"

"I was working late. There was a crisis at work and I'd been called into an emergency meeting." He turned to me. "That's why I didn't answer my phone when you called."

The officers seemed satisfied with his answers.

A short time later a pair of detectives arrived with a crime scene investigation team. The officers told us to stay in the kitchen, then they went into the living room to speak to the detectives. I held on to Marcus' hand like it was a lifeline, but didn't speak.

The detectives came into the kitchen to talk to us while the crime scene investigators took pictures and gathered other evidence in the living room.

"Ma'am, we'd like you to tell us exactly what happened tonight," Detective Towers said, pulling out a notepad and pen.

I told them how Trevor had come over to play with Natalie like he had been doing for the last few weeks, and at first everything was fine, but then he suddenly announced he was going to keep the baby. Then after making me put the dog out, he punched me in the head, which knocked me out. When I'd woken, my hands and feet were tied, but I was able to get the ropes off.

"Why didn't you call the police once you were free?"

"Maybe I should have, but I had an idea of how to get him to bring Natalie back." I paused, reliving the despair I'd felt when I'd realized Trevor had taken Natalie.

"Go on."

Pulling myself back to the present, I told them about finding the SD card and digging up the money and how I'd thought if I told Trevor about the money, he would be willing to give me Natalie back.

"Then what happened?" Detective Towers asked.

I told them how Trevor had agreed to trade the baby for the money and told me to meet him at the park, and what had happened there.

"Why did you come back to the house?"

"I don't know. I was in a panic and I didn't realize I'd left the keys to my car at the park."

"What happened when you got to the house?"

I recounted what had happened. When I got to the part where Trevor was strangling me, I felt Marcus' hand tighten on mine. "I knew I was going to die," I said, tears filling my eyes. "But then Greta came running through the front door and saved me."

"Is that Greta that I hear barking?" Detective Towers asked.

"Yes, I put her in my room so she wouldn't get in the way."

"What kind of dog is she?"

"A German Shepherd."

"And where is the money that you mentioned?" Towers asked.

"I don't know. I guess in my car."

"Let's go take a look," Towers said.

They followed me out to my car. Trevor had left the keys in the ignition. Detective Towers took them out and opened the trunk where we found the gym bag.

"And you don't know where the money originally came from?"

I shook my head. "It was buried where Trevor had put it."

Towers took the bag out of the trunk. "We'll need to do some investigating, but if it legitimately belonged to your husband, we'll give it back to you.

I almost told them I didn't want to have anything to do with it, but decided to keep my thoughts to myself.

We went back into the house and more people arrived. One of them was the coroner and he took Trevor's body away. Then a tow truck came and took Trevor's car. A third vehicle came. It was animal control.

"Why is animal control here?" I asked Detective Towers, feeling panicked about what they would do to Greta.

"It's just routine to test her for rabies. After the investigation you should get her back."

I wasn't sure if I believed him. I'd heard of cases where a dog was put down after attacking a person. "How can you be sure?"

"It seems pretty clear that she was defending you from an attempted murder. I think in this case you'll be able to keep her," he said.

Feeling somewhat assured, I went upstairs, first putting a sleeping Natalie in her crib, then getting Greta from my room and bringing her downstairs.

The man from animal control took her out to his truck and I watched as he put her in the back and drove away. Tears pushed their way into my eyes and I swallowed hard to keep from crying.

Eventually the crime investigation team finished gathering the evidence and left. Detective Towers and his partner walked out to their car.

"We'll be in touch," he said as he and his partner got into their car and drove away.

Marcus walked with me back into the house. I was exhausted, but still in shock about what had happened. He sat with me on the couch.

"Do you want to talk about it?" Marcus asked. "Or do you want to go to sleep?"

"I just can't believe he's dead," I said. Though Trevor had taken my baby and tried to kill me, I was saddened by his death. He had been my husband and there had been a time when I loved him.

"I'm really sorry this happened," Marcus said, taking my hand.

The warmth from his hand warmed me. I felt so cold. "He told me he was going to give my baby to his girlfriend."

"I heard you saying something about that to the detectives, but I didn't understand what that was all about."

"There was this girl named Amanda that he was always flirting with before we started dating and I guess when I left they got together. Apparently she can't have children of her own so he promised her he would get Natalie and give her to her." I stopped as my voice broke. Marcus put his arms around me and I leaned against him.

"It's okay. Everything's okay now," he murmured in my ear.

We sat that way for several minutes and I felt myself drifting to sleep.

"I'll carry you upstairs, Lily," Marcus whispered.

I nodded as he lifted me in his arms and carried me up the stairs. He set me on my bed and helped me take off my shoes before tucking me in.

Suddenly my eyes flew open. "What about the door?"

"Don't worry. I'll stay in the living room while you sleep and as soon as the hardware store opens, I'll put in a new door."

"Oh, Marcus," I said, as exhaustion overtook me. "You're wonderful."

Late the next morning I woke up feeling somewhat rested. The first time Natalie had cried after I'd gone to bed, I'd brought her into bed with me and she slept next to me now. Stroking her head, I smiled at my beautiful baby, then felt my heart clench as I thought about how close I had come to losing her to Trevor.

I was having trouble accepting the fact the Trevor was dead. It was ironic actually. Everyone had believed I was a widow and now I actually was. As I remembered the happy moments Trevor and I had spent, sadness washed over me and I shed tears for the man he could have been. Though I was glad he wouldn't be able to threaten me or Natalie anymore, I was deeply saddened that his life had to end when he was so young.

In my mind I recounted all that had happened in the last twenty-four hours. Even though it ended in tragedy, I felt proud that I had been able to defend myself as well as I had. And Greta was my hero. But how had she gotten out of the backyard?

I climbed out of bed and went into the bathroom. As I looked in the mirror I saw a ring of bruises beginning to form on my neck. After showering I put on a turtleneck, then changed Natalie and fed her. Carrying her in my arms, I went downstairs.

The front door was still broken, but mostly closed, keeping out the majority of the cold air. Marcus was asleep on the couch, a blanket pulled up to his chin. I smiled, grateful to have him in my life. Though we'd had a few rocky moments, he'd been there at the most important times and he was becoming a good friend. I left him to sleep, then set Natalie in her baby seat while I made breakfast.

As I waited for the first batch of pancakes to cook, I had a thought. Pulling open the silverware drawer, I lifted the tray and looked underneath. The paper where I'd written the alarm security code was gone. Trevor must have taken it when I was unconscious, I realized. Again, I wondered what he had planned on doing. He would have already taken the baby at that point, so why did he need to disable the alarm? Was he planning on coming back and getting rid of me? The idea filled me with horror. Although his death was terrible, I was grateful I had survived.

Closing the drawer, I pushed the thoughts aside, not wanting to speculate on what might have happened. What actually happened was awful enough.

When the pancakes were ready, I gently shook Marcus and invited him to eat. He stretched, then sat up on the couch. "Is it time to get up already?" he asked.

I laughed. "Only if you want some of my delicious pancakes."

"I definitely do."

We sat together at the table and ate a leisurely breakfast. As we finished eating, I thought about Greta and hoped I would have her back soon. "One thing that's been bothering me, Marcus," I said as I carried my plate into the kitchen. "How did Greta get out of the backyard? She's never gotten out before."

"Let's see if we can find out." He pushed away from the table.

Taking Natalie out of her baby seat, I followed Marcus as he went into the backyard and walked to the gate. It hung open. We looked at the latch and saw it had been broken.

"I'll bet Trevor broke that at some point last night," I said. "He was probably in a big hurry and didn't realize he'd broken it." I paused. "I wonder why he was even back here."

"Maybe he was looking for the breaker box to cut your power."

"Yeah. Maybe he thought it would keep the alarm from working." I controlled a shudder as I recalled the panic I'd felt when I'd realized the alarm wasn't working. "But he disabled it anyway."

"Well, I guess I'll fix the gate latch when I fix the front door," Marcus said.

I smiled. "What would I do without you to fix all these things?"

He grinned back. "I guess you'd be living in a broken down old house."

Later that day Marcus had fixed both the front door and the gate. I had the alarm company come out and fix the alarm. They told me it looked like the wire had been cut, which would normally set off the alarm, but then Trevor had apparently punched in the code, which kept the alarm company from knowing there was a problem.

Ten days later the man from animal control brought Greta back, saying she'd passed the rabies quarantine. She leapt from the back of the truck and rushed up to me, her tail wagging.

"You're such a good girl," I said as I squatted next to her and wrapped my arms around her.

Over the next few weeks Marcus spent more and more time at my place. Though it had taken him a little while, eventually he became comfortable holding Natalie and began to really enjoy playing with her.

The detectives finished their investigation and concluded that I had rightfully used self-defense and that Greta was not a threat. They had also discovered that the two hundred thousand dollars Rob and Trevor had buried was money they had won gambling. They gave half of it to Rob and the other half to me, with the understanding that I would have to pay taxes on it. I really didn't want to have anything to do with it, but I decided it should benefit Natalie, so I placed it in a trust for her to receive when she grew up.

When they'd asked Rob why they had buried it, he had said they'd been drinking and all he remembered was having the money and then it was gone and Trevor had claimed he'd lost it gambling.

As time went on, Marcus and I developed a strong bond, but neither one of us wanted to rush in to anything. We were both still trying to recover from past relationships and just wanted to enjoy spending time with each other without the pressure of expecting anything more.

One spring afternoon, when Natalie was four months old, she woke from a nap and I brought her down to the backyard. It was April and the California weather was perfect. I spread a blanket on the grass and lay her on her stomach in the middle of it as Greta picked up a ball and dropped it at my feet. Natalie lifted her head and watched as I threw the ball for Greta. A few minutes later Marcus came in through the back gate and joined in our play. I tossed him the ball and he threw it for Greta, then I sat on the blanket and put Natalie on my lap so she could see better.

As I watched Marcus throw the ball, he turned and smiled at me. My heart filled with warmth and I could see us being a family together. When I smiled back, he came over and sat next to me, wrapping his arms around me. Then he leaned close and nuzzled my neck.

"You smell good," he murmured.

I turned my face to his and our lips met. We kissed each other eagerly. When we pulled apart and gazed into each other's eyes, something new seemed to pass between us.

Maybe we're ready to take it to the next level after all, I thought as my smile widened. He smiled back, his incredible green eyes sparkling, and I knew he felt it too.

Lily's Story concludes in *Love At Last*.

Made in the USA
Lexington, KY
14 April 2014